Tales O'Lantern

Books 1, 2 and 3

A MARY O'REILLY SERIES SHORT STORY COLLECTION

by

Terri Reid

Tales Around the Jack O'Lantern 1 – A Mary O'Reilly Series Short Story

Copyright © 2014 by Terri Reid

Tales Around the Jack O'Lantern Two – A Mary O'Reilly Series Short Story

Copyright © 2015 by Terri Reid

Tales Around the Jack O'Lantern Three – A Mary O'Reilly Series Short Story

Copyright © 2016 by Terri Reid

Tales Around the Jack O' Lantern Collection

Copyright © 2016 by Terri Reid

Copyright © 2016 by Terri Reid

All rights reserved. Without limiting the rights under copyright reserved above, no part of this publication may be reproduced, stored in or introduced into a retrieval system, or transmitted, in any form, or by any means (electronic, mechanical, photocopying, recording, or otherwise) without the prior written permission of both the copyright owner and the above publisher of this book.

This is a work of fiction. Names, characters, places, brands, media, and incidents are either the product of the author's imagination or are used fictitiously. The author acknowledges the trademarked status and trademark owners of various products referenced in this work of fiction, which have been used without permission. The publication/ use of these trademarks is not authorized, associated with, or sponsored by the trademark owners.

The author would like to thank all those who have contributed to the creation of this book: Richard Reid, Sarah Powers, Jennifer Ellefson and Katie Solomon.

Happy Halloween!!!

Book One

Chapter One

(Ten years ago)

The candles in the jack-o-lanterns on the front porch were already burning low and the candy dish sitting on the hallway table in the O'Reilly's Chicago home had been refilled three times. The street lights were glowing brightly and most of the neighborhood goblins, ghouls and princesses had finished their Halloween ritual and were either tucked securely in their beds dreaming of candy corn and miniature-sized candy bars or actually sorting through their bounty from a successful rampage of trick-or-treating.

Mary O'Reilly, the youngest of the O'Reilly clan, had graduated from college at the end of the summer and was now enrolled in the Police Academy eagerly anticipating becoming a police officer in the Chicago Police Department like most of the other members of her family. She sat back in her favorite chair in their living room, an afghan tucked around her legs on the cool October night, and turned to the rest of her family. "Okay, it's time to get started," she announced.

Her brother Art, one of the twenty-three year-old twins, grabbed a handful of candy from the bowl and headed towards the couch.

"Arthur Patrick O'Reilly," Mary's mother, Margaret, scolded. "You leave that candy for the trick-or-treaters."

"Ma, it's already after nine," he argued, popping a piece in his mouth. "They should be home by now, not prowling the streets."

"It's only the teenagers out now, Ma," Sean O'Reilly, the oldest sibling in the group added, taking a few pieces from the bowl too. "And they shouldn't be knocking on doors anyway. They're too old."

Timothy O'Reilly, the large, bear of a man who was the father of the clan, chuckled, "I seem to recall the three of you eager and willing to take your little sister out door to door in hopes of getting some candy for yourselves when you were teenagers."

Tom, the other half of the twins, grinned. "Well, it was better than stealing candy away from Mary," he laughed, taking a seat next to Art and swiping some of his candy. "And besides, it was a public service. The neighbors didn't want to be left with all that extra candy."

"You're no better now than you were then," Margaret teased gently.

"Except now we help buy the candy," Sean replied.

"Okay, enough about candy," Mary said. "We have some serious business here. The annual

O'Reilly ghost story night is about to begin. Everyone needs to settle in."

Sean walked over to the doorway and dimmed the lights while Timothy lit the candle in the large jack-o-lantern sitting on the coffee table between them. They all took their seats in the living room, the light from the candle flickering wildly around on the walls. Margaret carried in a tray filled with cups of hot apple cider and plates of pumpkin bars and placed it next to the jack-o-lantern. While her family helped themselves, she took her place in the old rocking chair and took a deep breath. "Well, I believe it's my turn to start the story telling," she began. "I've been thinking about what I'd share for a while now. And, with Mary in the Police Academy, I thought it was time I shared a story your father and I both experienced that I haven't mentioned before."

She was silent for a moment. The house was also silent; the only sound to be heard was the slight tick-tock of the clock in the hallway. The candle now burned brightly, only wavering slightly, filling the room with a soft glow. The eyes of all of the members of the O'Reilly family turned to the shadowed face of their mother. And she began her story.

Chapter Two

It was a night like many others in the life of the wife of a police officer, alone and worried. Margaret O'Reilly had done the dishes, put her daughter Mary to bed and even read her a story. But throughout the evening she'd been bothered by a nagging fear. It was the kind of fear that eats at your heart and digs at your nerves. Most nights she was able to chalk it up to an overactive imagination, but this night she jumped every time a car drove by and stared at the phone for minutes on end, waiting for it to ring. Waiting for *that* message from the captain, offering his sincerest regrets.

She put in another load of laundry and took the last one out of the dryer. Folding towels was mindless enough that she could do it and not think about it. But even from the laundry room off the kitchen, she kept glancing to the phone on the wall, waiting for it to ring, praying it would not.

She kept calling herself a fool. Kept telling herself that he was fine. But, she knew in her heart of hearts, that something really was wrong.

Finally, she finished the laundry and started pacing in the kitchen. She glanced up at the clock and the panic increased. He should have been home by now. Or, he should have called to tell her he was going to be late. That was the rule. The only rule. If he was fine, but was going to be late, he had to call. Had to stop her from worrying.

Walking over to the phone, she put her hand on the receiver. She didn't really want to call, didn't want to make it look like she was checking up on him. But she had to know.

"Margie?"

The voice from the other side of the room startled her and she jumped, sending the receiver crashing to the ground. Breathing a sigh of relief, she saw it was John Polichek, Tim's partner, standing in the kitchen doorway. "Johnny," she said, and then she realized it was just John and not Tim and the fear that had been weaving through her gut froze solid. "Timmy?"

"Hey, sorry, don't worry," John said. "Tim's fine. I promise."

A wave of overwhelming relief washed over her. She swallowed twice before she could speak. "Really?" He's fine?" she stammered.

John smiled at her and nodded. "Yeah, we walked into a little trouble down on the East side, but Tim's fine," he said. "They sent him to the hospital, to get a couple of stitches. But, he's good. I just wanted to stop by here, 'cause I knew you would be worried."

Exhaling slowly, she leaned against the wall, trying to control the flood of emotions and the tears. "Thank you, Johnny," she said, picking up a kitchen towel from the counter and wiping her eyes. "You're right, I was worried."

"Yeah, that's what I thought," he said. "You're a good wife. And Tim's the best partner a guy could ever have."

She smiled. "I won't tell him you said that," she said, surprised that she could tease him. "We wouldn't want it to go to his head."

Johnny smiled and nodded. "Yeah, well, just this time you can let him know what I said," he replied.

She kicked against the receiver on the floor and shook her head. "I guess I'd better pick this up in case he decides to call," she bent down and turned to place the phone back on the hook. "Would you like some coffee…"

She turned, but Johnny was no longer near the kitchen door. "Johnny?" she called out.

Walking through the kitchen and into the hall, she saw that the bathroom door was open, so he hadn't gone in there. Maybe he had to get back to the station. Maybe he mentioned it, but she didn't hear him when she was turned away to get the phone. She hurried to the door to look for his car, but no one was on the street. Shrugging, she went back to the kitchen, her heart lightened and waited for Timmy to get home.

As soon as his car turned down the street, she was out of her chair and hurrying for the door. When he opened it, his arm wrapped in a cast and a bandage over his forehead, she moved forward into his arms. He didn't say a word, just held her against him, each seeking and giving the comfort they needed. After a few moments, she leaned back, running her hands gently up to his shoulders. "How are you?" she asked.

He placed a kiss on her forehead. "I'm good," he said softly. "I'm fine. I got hurt and had to go to the hospital."

She nodded. "I know," she said, leaning into his arms again.

"You know?" he asked. "I told them not to call you. I told them you'd be worried sick."

She shook her head. "No, no one called," she explained, her head nestled against his chest. "Johnny stopped by and told me that you were okay. He said he knew I'd worry, so he wanted to tell me himself." She smiled. "He also said that you are the best partner a guy could have."

She heard the sharp intake of breath and she felt him stiffen beneath her. Pulling away, she looked up into his eyes and saw the tears. "What?" she asked frantically. "What?"

"Johnny," he replied haltingly. "Johnny didn't…"

"Did something happen to him on the way back to the station?" she demanded. "He was just here…"

He shook his head and placed his forehead against hers. "Johnny was with me when we walked into the ambush," he explained hoarsely. "He was the first guy in. He…he didn't make it."

Chapter Three

There was silence once again in the living room when Margaret finished and wiped the tears from her cheeks. "He was a good man," she said.

Tim nodded. "Aye, he was," he replied. "And knew what it was to be a good partner. Sometimes I still feel him watching over me."

"Do you think that's possible?" Mary asked. "Ghosts watching over people? Ghosts being here on the earth?"

Tim took a deep breath and nodded. "I do, yes," he said. "And, actually, when I was a young lad growing up in Chicago I had an experience that caused me never to doubt that there is a world out there that few understand. And, since I believe it's my turn, I'll share the story with the rest of you."

The day had finally arrived, twelve-year-old Timmy O'Reilly was old enough to have his own paper route. How he'd envied those other boys with their pockets filled with change, buying the latest comics books or stopping for a treat at the ice cream parlor. He was at last, a working man.

He had thought of nothing else that day in school. He got his knuckles rapped twice by his teacher, a nun with a very sour disposition, for not paying attention to the board work. But all he could think about was the stack of papers that would be waiting for him when he got home that afternoon.

He ran all the way, crisp autumn leaves crunching beneath his shoes, the crisp wind turning his cheeks pinks and blowing his hair off his face. Taking the front steps two at a time, he dashed through the front door calling to his mother, "Are they here yet?"

Coming from the back of the house, his mother smiled at her eager son. "Yes, Timmy, they are," she said. "Now, why don't you take a moment and study your route, then we can fold the papers and pack them in your bag."

Timmy shook his head. "No, we have to fold them right away," he replied. "The circulation manager told me that I had to be real quick. So, let's fold them and I can learn the route on the way."

Shaking her head, but allowing her son to lead the way in his new business venture, Mrs. O'Reilly sat on the living room floor and began to fold the papers and pack them neatly in the large canvas bag with the paper's name emblazoned on the side. With both of them working, side by side, the bag was soon filled and Timmy was ready to go. With the canvas bag handle looped around his shoulders and the bag resting on his back fender, he straddled his bike, route addresses in hand and started off. "Bye Mom," he called, his face glowing with excitement. "I'll be home for supper." He only said that because it was something his father had said and it made him feel like a real working man.

"Good-bye dear," she replied, biting back a smile. "Good luck with your route and remember, you are representing the paper."

Pushing off and pedaling into the street, he thought about his mother's last words. He was representing the paper now. He wasn't just Timmy O'Reilly; he was part of the Chicago Beacon. He needed to be sure he remembered that.

He biked the four blocks to his first street. It was like all of the streets in his neighborhood, tree-lined and residential, with neat little Chicago bungalows lining the street. The porches already had decorations in place for the celebration of Halloween at the end of the week. The jack-o-lanterns were carved and stared at him with dark, vacant eyes and smiles, awaiting the candles that would light them up. Ghosts, scarecrows and witches also shared the porches with the carved pumpkins, awaiting the ghouls and goblins with the bags for trick or treating. Timmy already had his costume planned; he was going as a policeman, the only costume he ever wore.

Slowing at the porch of the first customer, he realized it was the home of a classmate. Jenny Callahan, one of the cutest girls in the seventh grade. She stood next to the railing and watched him. He felt sweat pool between his shoulders and his hand got a little clammy. If he messed this one up, the whole school would know about it. Taking a deep breath, he reached for a paper and threw it on the porch. He'd been practicing his throw for several weeks, and it paid off when the paper hit the porch and slid to land next to the welcome mat near the front door. "Cool," he said, his grin broadening. "This is going to be great."

Jenny smiled at him, then bent and picked up the paper. "Wait, Timmy," she called, walking into her house. Confused, he waited. Did he do something wrong? A moment later she walked out and came down the stairs. She handed him a shiny dime. "My mom always tips our newspaper boys," she said.

Timmy smiled back at her and stuffed the dime in his pocket. "Wow, thanks," he said. "Thanks a lot."

Yeah, this was going to be a great job, Timmy thought as he pedaled away from Jenny's house. He continued down the street, each paper landing precisely where he wanted it to go. And as he continued his route, the sky darkened, the streets became less occupied and he could tell that night was settling in. The final street on his route was a dead-end, so he decided he would deliver to one side of the street, then the house at the end of the cul-de-sac, finish with the other side of the street and finally go home.

The trees on this particular street were spaced closer to each other and their overhanging branches formed a tunnel down the middle of the narrow street. The sidewalks were in disrepair and often leaned to the side or were crumbled in the middle. He rode his bike carefully, not wanting to fall over. Timmy glanced quickly down the sidewalk, he couldn't remember ever coming down this street before.

As he approached the first porch, he picked up the next paper, waited until the next porch came into range and fired it off. Slap. Slide. Perfect hit. Even in the dimming light, he had good aim. He continued with the next six houses and then came to last house at the dead end. The sidewalk here was nearly non-existent and the house was set away from the street, so he couldn't see the porch. He laid his bike against the tall, black wrought-iron fence at the edge of the property. Weeds, bushes and dried chrysanthemums encased the fence and nearly swallowed Timmy's bike. Pulling a paper out of the bag, he walked to the tall gate, pushed it open and froze.

The old house reminded him of the sidewalk, leaning and dilapidated. The windows were dark and what was left of the porch was leaning dangerously in the opposite direction of the rest of the house. He started to step back, away from the gate and back to his bike. But then he remembered his mother's words. He was a representative of the paper and it was his job to deliver the news.

Swallowing his fears, he took a deep breath and walked forward towards the house. The leaves under his feet crunched with such noise he wondered if they were really corn flakes instead of leaves. The air around him seemed to be still and heavy. It was harder to breathe, but that could have been because his heart was beating so quickly.

As he placed his foot on the first step he heard a rustling sound in the overgrowth next to the house and he nearly stepped back. Then he looked down at the paper in his hand, and placed his next foot on the step. Looking around the porch, he tried to find a safe place to put the paper. But where the porch was not rotted away, it was covered with spider webs or thick vines. He had no other choice than to deliver it in person.

The wooden screen door lay haphazardly against its frame, the screening hanging loosely down the side. He put this hand through the hole and knocked on the old front door. A dim glow appeared in the windows next to the door and Timmy breathed a sigh of relief. *Good! Someone was home.*

Timmy counted to sixty-three times before the knob on the other side of the door rattled and the door slowly opened. A thin, wrinkled face peeked out from the narrow space between the door and frame. "Hello?" the parched voice whispered. "What do you want?"

Clearing his throat several times to get rid of the panic, Timmy took his cap off his head to be polite and finally said, "I'm here with your paper." Lifting the said object up for the thin man to see.

Eyes almost too wide for their sockets followed the movement. "Paper?" he croaked.

Nodding eagerly, Timmy handed it to him. "Yes, it's today's copy of the Chicago Beacon," he replied. "I'm your new paperboy."

A long, thin hand reached out and grasped the paper, slowly pulling it back into the house, but at the last moment, the paper slipped from his grasp and tumbled to the floor. Dropping his hat, Timmy dove for the paper and caught it before it disappeared into one of the holes in the porch. "Here you are," he said, offering the paper again.

The old face stared at him for a moment longer and then nearly cracked in half with a wide smile. "Thank you, boy," he whispered.

"You're welcome, sir," Timmy replied. "Um, have a nice evening."

The old man nodded slowly and then closed the door.

Breathing a sigh of relief, Timmy walked down the stairs and stepped onto the sidewalk. The rustling in the overgrown lawn intensified and all he could imagine were big, hairy rats waiting to grab hold of him and pull him under. Tossing caution to the wind, he ran down the sidewalk and pushed the gate closed firmly behind him.

Pulling his bike from the bushes, he hopped back on it and hurried down the street, delivering the rest of the papers. When he got to the very last house on his route, he reached in the bag and, to his surprise, found no more papers.

There had to be a mistake. He had enough papers for every house on his route.

Pedaling his bike next to a streetlight, he pulled out the paper with the route. He counted the addresses on the street; there was one less subscriber than houses on the street. Studying it, he realized the old house with the iron fence had not been a subscriber. He'd given them a free paper. He thought for a moment about going back there, but only for a moment. There was no way he was going back through that yard in the dark. But, it was his fault, he hadn't checked his route before.

He dug into his pants pocket and pulled out the shiny dime. He knew what he had to do. He rode out of the dead end street and over a block to a metal newspaper box on the corner, inserted his dime and pulled out the paper he needed. In a few minutes, the paper was delivered and he was on his way back home.

"Hey, Mom, I'm home," he said, walking through the front door.

"How'd it go?" she asked, looking up from setting the dining room table for dinner.

"Good," he replied. "But there's a lot to this newspaper business."

She smiled at him. "I'm sure there is," she agreed, and then she paused and looked at him. "Where's your hat?"

He moaned and closed his eyes. He knew exactly where he'd lost it, on the rickety porch when he'd dived to catch the paper. "I left it at one of the houses on my route," he confessed. "I'll leave early for school in the morning and get it."

Maybe the house wouldn't be as scary in the daytime.

The following morning, Timmy rode his bike back down the route from the night before. *It does make a difference coming during the daytime*, he thought as he pedaled down the dead-end street, *things look a lot less scary with sunshine on them.*

Although, he had to admit, the fence at the end of the street didn't look a whole lot better. He leaned his bike against the fence again, as he had done the night before and walked over to the gate. But this time he saw something he'd missed the night before. A large sign was attached to the middle of the gate. "Condemned – Do Not Enter"

How did he miss that?

He hated to ignore the sign, but his hat was in there and, besides, it really hadn't been all that bad last night.

He pushed the gate as far as he could, this time there was a chain around the gate and the post, and he slipped through. He walked a couple of steps and froze. The house was gone. All that was left was charred remains. The porch was lying on the ground in pieces. What few windows that were left were shattered and there was no roof, only a burnt and gaping hole.

Timmy shook his head. He could tell by the vines growing up the side of the house, the fire had happened a long time ago, not since last night.

He took a step back, towards the gate, when something hanging on a post near the house caught his eye. His hat. Someone had placed his hat up where he could find it. It took him a moment to get his legs to move, but when he could he ran, grabbed his hat and sped back to the gate.

As he pushed himself back through the narrow opening, he was sure he felt someone touch his shoulder and whisper, "Thank you, boy."

Chapter Four

A cold breeze drifted through the room and the candle's flame flickered wildly sending shadows dancing on the walls. Mary shivered and pulled the afghan closer in the darkened room, picturing the old man her father had described. She looked across the room and jumped, muffling a scream as she quickly realized the pale, white specters sitting across the room were actually her twin brothers holding flashlights under their chin. "Not funny," she criticized.

Chuckling, they gave each other high-fives and grabbed more candy from the bowl. "Not another bite of candy," their mother warned, instantly staying their hands. Then her voice warmed greatly. "Not until you share a story."

The young men looked at each other and, in the uncanny way of twins, communicated without speaking and just nodded. Then, two voices taking turns and nearly speaking as one, they shared their story.

The two Marines pushed through the thick forest, their weapons drawn and their senses alert. They had become separated from their unit during a skirmish with the opposition force but because of the unspoken bond they had shared from the womb, they were still together. They had been fighting in a valley and, between the bluffs and dense vegetation, had no way to see if they were in a safe spot or if the enemy troops were on their trail.

They clambered up a hill, hiding behind the large boulders and primeval trees. This forest in Southern Europe was older than any building in the United States and the Irish twins from Chicago could feel the ancient power emanating from it. "Where do you think we are?" the younger twin, Tom, asked his older brother, Art, in a whisper.

"I think we're about six clicks from the main road," Art replied softly, then seeing the look of frustration on Tom's face added, "Like three miles."

Tom grinned briefly. "Thanks," he said. "I don't know why they can't just use miles."

They hunkered down behind a huge boulder and listened to the sounds of artillery fire in the distance. "Sounds like it might be coming closer," Art finally said softly.

"Yeah, but who's coming closer?" Tom asked.

"Good question," Art replied.

They both took drinks from their water bottles, mimicking each other's actions unconsciously and then wiped an arm across each face in twin synchronicity. Synchronicity so strong that the military, who normally separated brothers, decided that this time it would be a boon for the Special Forces they served for them to be together. "Which way?" Art asked Tom.

Tom angled his head in the direction away from the noise of the fighting. "If we can get through this valley and up on one of the bluffs, we'll be able to get a better idea of where our guys are," he said. "And we might be in a better position to help them."

Pulling their helmet back onto their heads, they moved slowly around the boulder, staying low and headed down into the underbrush towards the edge of the forest. About a half mile later, Art put his hand on Tom's shoulder to stop him.

Tom turned and was about to speak when the quick shake of Art's head stopped him. Instantly alert he listened intently and heard it too. In the distance, coming from the opposite direction of the fighting, were the sounds of voices.

"Soldiers?" Tom whispered.

Art shook his head again. "Too unguarded," he said. "It has to be civilians."

"We've got to warn them a battle is coming to their neighborhood," Tom said.

Art nodded in agreement.

Doubling their pace, but still trying to move stealthily through the brush, they covered another half mile in no time. There was a clearing a few yards ahead of them, so they stopped and listened again. This time the sounds were clearer.

"Kids," Tom said, grimacing. "Dammit, those are kids' voices."

"I remember from the recon map there was an orphanage in the area," Art said. "We gotta get them out of there."

They moved to the edge of the forest and stopped. "There it is," Tom said, pointing to a large brick building on the top of a hill over a half of a mile away.

Art looked up and down the tree line next to where they stood. "If we run out into that field, we're sitting ducks," he said. "There is no protection."

They looked into each other's eyes and understood what they had to do. In one quick motion, they put their arms around each other in a quick hug, then stepped back, turned and ran into the field. The noise from the artillery was closer than before and they could feel the earth shaking from explosions from larger weapons, but they continued to run.

In the distance they could hear the thrumming of a fighter jet and prayed, if it was one of theirs, it would recognize them and they wouldn't become casualties of friendly fire.

Their feet beat against the dusty, hard ground of the field. Their hearts pounding in their throats, their eyes focused on the base of the hill. Together, step by step, they ran, praying they would still be alive at the end of the day.

They dove into the brush at the base of the hill, breathing heavily and waiting for a moment to see if sniper fire would follow them in. Finally, as their breathing slowed and their hearts stopped pounding, they heard them again. The children. But this time, they were singing.

"What the hell?" Tom asked, standing and moving towards the stone steps at the bottom of the hill. "What kind of teacher has choir practice when they hear mortar shells exploding in the vicinity?"

"Why aren't those kids in a bomb shelter?" Art asked, finishing his brother's thoughts.

They jogged up the steps and rushed across the green lawn that led to the front of the large building. The song grew stronger as they neared; a haunting melody that was both a prayer and a lament.

Tom grabbed the door and Art covered him, his weapon ready. Tom pulled open the door and they both rushed inside. The music stopped.

The men stumbled back against the wall, too overcome to speak. There was no longer a school. All that was left was the front wall, a façade that covered the devastation of an attack that decimated both the building and its occupants. Scattered within the rubble of the building were the broken lifeless bodies of the children.

Oblivious to the sounds of war beyond the hill, the two brothers worked into the night digging a grave and carrying the little bodies to their final resting place. There were no adults found, so the brothers assumed the children had been left to fend for themselves as the war waged on around them. At the far end of the school, in the place that used to be a playground, freshly turned earth now protected the remains of the children who used to run and play. Art and Tom removed their helmets and bowed their heads. "Now I lay me down to sleep," Art began and Tom joined in, repeating the old prayer their mother had taught them as children. "I pray the Lord my soul to keep. His Love to guard me through the night, and wake me in the morning's light. Now I lay me down to sleep, I pray the Lord my soul to keep. Thy angels watch me through the night and keep me safe till morning's light."

Their voices cracked and they each took a deep, shuddering breath and continued with the final verse, "Now I lay me down to sleep, I pray the Lord my soul to keep. If I should die before I wake, I pray the Lord, my soul to take."

Then, exhausted, the brothers stumbled to the lone wall and fell asleep under its shelter.

The sounds of an approaching helicopter woke them in the early dawn. Looking up, they saw a Blackhawk circling the field in front of the school for a place to land. Grabbing their gear, they ran from the shelter towards their comrades.

"How you do it?" asked the Marine who helped them climb into the chopper.

"Do what?" Art asked.

"Send up that beacon?"

"Beacon?" Tom asked.

"Yeah, it was like a beam of white light shooting straight up from your location. It lasted for about ten minutes," the Marine said. "Long enough for us to figure out where you were and get you out before you were overrun. It was like a miracle."

"Yeah, something like that," Art said.

"Yeah, just like that," Tom added.

Chapter Five

"How come you never told us about this before tonight?" Sean asked his brothers.

They both shrugged. "It wasn't time yet," Art said.

"Yeah, tonight, it was the right time," Tom added.

A soft, sniffling noise was heard coming from their mother's direction.

"Hey, we didn't tell it to make you cry, Ma," Tom said.

"I'm not crying at all," Margaret contended. "It's a bit of a cold I've had for a day or so."

"Well, my story will scare the snot right out of you," Sean announced.

"Sean," his mother reprimanded.

"Sorry, Ma," he said, with a very unrepentant tone while his brothers snickered in the dark.

"I was a rookie in the force," he began. "And it was just about Halloween…"

The rookies always got the worst beats and even though Sean O'Reilly was fifth generation

Chicago cop, there were no exceptions. So, he walked the graveyard shift around Lincoln Park on the north side of the city, next to the lake. Although Lincoln Park stretched for over seven miles along Chicago's lakefront, Sean's area was twelve hundred acres of grass, trees, bike paths, jogging paths, museums and even a zoo that bordered Diversey Parkway on the north and North Avenue on the south. During the day, this area was a mecca of activity for families on picnics, joggers running alongside the lake and buses filled with children going on field trips. At night, it was a mugger's paradise. This was why Sean O'Reilly was required to walk the nearly two square miles over and over and over again every night.

With the leather band of his flashlight swinging slowly from his hand as he walked, Sean started on the farthest north portion of the park and followed the bike path along Stockton Drive, passing by the statues, the softball diamonds, the benches and the landscaping. After exploring this part of Chicago by foot for over a month, he had become familiar with every dark shadow and each unique sound. He experienced, in his own mind, a symphony of the lake shore at night. The waves slapping the rocks were the percussion, the sailboats rubbing against their moorings created the high-pitch cry of stringed instruments, the breeze whipping through the tall masts of the sailboats in the harbor were the wind instruments and the honking from the cars on Lake Shore Drive were the brass. Occasionally, especially if the moon were full, some of the animals from Lincoln Park Zoo would be featured as guest soloists, leaving their haunting cries echoing throughout the park.

Sean even got to know the difference between the sound of a squirrel in the brush and the sound of a rat searching for food. He avoided them both, he was a cat person.

It was on one of those nights, when the moon was full and the leaves had nearly all fallen off the trees, that he met August. The old man sitting on the park bench in the dark startled him at first and then concerned him. “Excuse me, sir,” Sean said as he approached the motionless man. “Are you okay?”

It took a moment for the man to respond; he stared at Sean and shook his head twice, as if he couldn’t quite believe someone was speaking to him. “I beg your pardon,” the man replied. “Were you speaking to me?”

Nodding, Sean sat down next to the fellow. He was not very tall, rather plump and squinted, as if he’d lost his glasses. What was left of his hair was thin, white and tossed over his bald head in one of the worst comb-overs Sean had ever seen. “Yes, I was speaking to you,” Sean said, keeping his voice gentle so as not to startle the elderly gentleman.

“Oh, well, then let me respond. I am quite well, thank you.”

Sean smiled. “I’m Sean O’Reilly,” he said.

“Oh, how do you do,” the man replied with a wide smile. “I’m Augustin Bates. Please call me August.”

“I don’t believe I’ve seen you here before,” Sean said.

“Really?” August replied, surprised. “Well, that’s funny. This is where I spend most of my evenings.”

“Well, perhaps that’s the problem,” Sean said, wondering if the old man had lost track of time. “It’s nearly one o’clock in the morning. Not evening at all.”

The old man met Sean’s eyes with a twinkle in his own. “No, not evening at all,” he replied with a chuckle. “More like the witching hours to be quite precise.”

“I thought the witching hour was midnight,” Sean said.

August shook his head. “Oh, no, historically any time between midnight and three in the morning were known as the witching hours.”

Sean nodded slowly. “So, you’re into history?” he asked.

"Yes. Yes, I am very fond of history," August replied, "Especially the history of this part of the city. It has quite a colorful history."

"Well, I would love to hear more," Sean said, deciding the old man was harmless and seemed to be in full possession of his faculties. "But I really have to continue to patrol."

Sean stood and, surprisingly, the little man stood too. "Do you mind if I walk along with you?" he asked. "I promise not to be a bother."

"No problem," Sean said. "And maybe you could share a little of that history of yours with me. It'll help me to get to know Lincoln Park a little better."

"It would be my pleasure," August replied.

They walked along in silence for a few minutes and then the old man cleared his throat. "Well, the first thing you should know about the park is that it was once a cemetery," he said.

"No!" Sean said, halting and looking at his companion with disbelief. "A cemetery."

"Yes, it was the very first city cemetery," he replied. "Back when the city didn't stretch quite as far to the north."

"Was it a big cemetery?" Sean asked, looking down at the ground below his feet.

"Oh, yes," August replied. "It stretched from Diversey Parkway to North Avenue and held the bodies of thousands of the dear departed. They were from all walks of life. There were those who died from the cholera epidemic, those who were just poor who were buried in Potter's Field, those who actually bought cemetery plots for families members and the soldiers."

"Soldiers?" Sean asked.

August nodded sadly. "There were six thousand Confederate soldiers who died in Camp Douglas whose bodies were buried here too," he replied.

"Six thousand soldiers," Sean repeated, surprised at the number. "How many people were buried in the park?"

"About thirty-five thousand," August replied, shaking his head. Then he leaned in and whispered. "And some of them are still here."

A cold chill ran down his spine and he took a deep breath. "What do you mean, still here?"

"Well, the folks in the city decided that they didn't want the bodies this close to the water, they said it was a health hazard," August said, contempt in his voice. "If you ask me, they just didn't like the idea of a graveyard built near where they wanted to build all their fancy new homes."

"So, where did they put the bodies?" Sean asked.

August began walking again and Sean followed along. "Well," August said, picking up his cane and pointing it in a westward direction. "Most of the bodies were moved over to Graceland cemetery. They got fine new plots and markers there. The city did a fine job of making sure people were satisfied with the move."

He continued to walk, moving further into the park. "But the sexton of the park," he began, and then he stopped and looked at Sean. "That was the fellow who was in charge of the cemetery. He dug the graves and kept things neat and clean. He ran the place."

"The sexton," Sean repeated.

August nodded with a smile. "Yes, the sexton was responsible for the graves of all those who were buried," he said, walking down a narrow path that was surrounded by trees on both sides. "And he knew that they didn't take them all. They didn't move them. They just moved the important ones and left thousands of bodies here under the park. No markers, no gravestones, no one to remember them."

Sean shook his head. "No, someone remembered them," he replied. "It seems to me that any sexton worth his title would have remembered them no matter if they were rich or poor."

August turned to Sean and smiled brightly. "You are a bright young man," he said. "And you do understand. Yes. Yes, the sexton would remember."

"But, what I don't understand is how you know all those graves weren't moved," Sean said.

The air grew still and heavy. The noise from Lake Shore Drive faded away and the whining from the boats in the pier intensified for a moment, as if thousands of lost souls had cried out.

August met Sean's eyes and his smile turned sad. "Because, my dear, young man, I'm still here." And then he vanished from sight.

Chapter Six

"The next morning, when I got off shift, I went onto the computer," Sean added. "And sure enough, Augustus Bates had been the City Sexton during the time the old City Cemetery had been closed down."

"Did you ever see him again?" Mary asked.

"A couple of times I thought I caught a glimpse of him," he admitted. "And I thought he waved at me. But it was always dark, so I guess I could have imagined it."

"But you don't think so, do you?" Mary asked.

Sean paused for a moment and then shook his head. "No, I think what I saw was real," he said. "I never thought I'd actually believe in ghosts. But there it is."

Mary nodded. "Yes, there it is," she repeated. "And I never thought I would believe in ghosts either. But sometimes—"

She looked over at her mother and smiled shyly. "So what is the statute of limitations on not quite telling your parents the truth?"

Margaret studied her daughter for a moment and then sighed loudly. "Seeing that it's Halloween, you have one free pass," she replied.

"Thank you, Ma," Mary said with a slight nod of her head. "So, let me tell you how I came to believe in ghosts."

The noon bell had just rung and the young girl stood in the doorway of her sixth-grade classroom watching the flurry of students, all dressed in the green and blue plaid of their Catholic school uniforms, rush towards the staircase that led to the lunch room on the ground level. She waited until their noise had died down before she pushed herself off the door jamb and made her way downstairs to eat her own lunch of peanut butter and jelly sandwich, homemade cookies, carrot sticks and ranch dip that her mother had lovingly prepared.

"How are you this morning, dear?"

Mary paused to smile at the elderly nun coming from one of the rooms at the end of the hall. It had become a daily occurrence for Mary to greet the woman every school day.

"I'm fine, Sister," she replied. "How are you?"

With a twinkle in her aging blue eyes the Sister would always smile at Mary and repeat the same phrase. "It's always a good day when you get to meet a friend. Have a good lunch, dear."

With a smile on her face, Mary would climb down the stairs to the lunchroom and wait in line to buy a carton of milk before she found an empty spot at one of the tables in the corner of the room.

But today was different. Once the milk was purchased, someone across the room called her name. "Mary! Mary O'Reilly! Come here and sit with us."

Mary looked over to see Janice Heppner standing at a table on the other side of the room, waving at her. Janice and her friends had been in Mary's class since first grade. Even then there had been a distinct separation of the girls who would be popular and the ones who wouldn't. Even back then Mary was one of the girls who ate alone and played alone at recess. She looked at the other girls at the table; their heads all turned in her direction and wondered if she had to strength to just walk away.

No. She had to admit that a part of her dearly wanted to be one of them. So, curiosity and peer pressure forced her feet to move her from the quiet side of the lunchroom to the table where Janice and her friends sat. They slid over and opened up a spot for her at the end of the bench. Putting her sack and milk down in front of her spot, Mary sat down.

"Hi Mary," Janice gushed. "Guess what? I'm having a Halloween party on Friday night."

Mary unwrapped the plastic from around her sandwich and picked up half. "That's nice," she replied before biting into it.

"Don't you want to know who's coming?" Janice asked.

Knowing that her name would not be on the list, Mary shrugged. "Sure," she said, and bit down again.

"Everyone who's cool is coming," Janice said.

Yes, Mary thought, *that would leave me out.*

"We were all thinking that it would be nice if you could come," Janice added.

Mary nearly choked on her next bite of sandwich. "Me?" she coughed.

Janice nodded her head. "Yes, and maybe your brothers could come with you."

Ah, here was the real purpose for the invitation, Mary sighed. Her twin brothers, Art and Tom, were several years older than she and they were star athletes at the high school. If Janice could get them to come to her party, she would have been in the same league as the high school popular girls.

"Yeah, well, they don't go to parties much," Mary hedged. "They mostly practice and work out."

"But it's Halloween night," Janice argued. "There wouldn't be any work outs on Halloween."

She had a point, Mary thought. However, she couldn't come up with a polite way to tell Janice that her brothers wouldn't be seen dead at a middle-school girl's party. "Well, I'll ask them and see if they want to come," she finally said.

The girls around the table burst into excited chatter about the twins, taking Mary's polite response as sure thing. Didn't any of these girls have brothers? Didn't they know the last thing older brothers wanted to do was anything that made their younger sister happy? Sighing, she took another bite of her sandwich, which now tasted a little like sawdust, and tried to keep a smile on her face.

"Oh," Janice announced as a polite afterthought. "Even if they can't, you know, come to my party. If you want to, you can just come by yourself."

# # #

Why is it, Mary wondered nervously as she stared at her costume in the mirror on Friday evening, *that when you want time to fly by it never does? But when you want it to just stand still, it flies by?*

She was dressed as witch; black stockings, black tulle skirt that went to her knees, a black turtleneck and a witch's hat. Her brown hair had been caught back in a bun and she actually had been allowed to wear make-up. Not the kind that made you look like a clown, but real make-up that accented your eyes and made your cheeks appear more distinct and rosy. She felt older and a little braver than normal, she felt sophisticated. The crowning accessory to her costume was the glittering, black domino mask. It was just beautiful in its simplicity; silver glitter and sparkling beads outlining the edges and the eye holes. It covered enough of her face that she was disguised.

"Mary, you need to hurry or you'll be late to the party," her mother called up the stairs.

She sighed. Her mother had been more excited than she was when Mary had told her about the invitation. She had gone shopping the next day to put together a costume that would make her daughter feel comfortable in the midst of the other girls.

"Coming," Mary called back. She slipped her jean jacket over her costume and jogged down the stairs.

"Oh, no, it's a lovely night. It's Indian summer," her mother said, sliding the jacket from Mary's shoulders. "You won't be needing that."

"But Mom, I'm more comfortable wearing it," Mary complained.

"Hiding inside it, I'd say," Margaret replied, with a no-nonsense look on her face. "You go to the party and have fun. You'll be the belle of the ball."

"Fine. Thanks, Mom," Mary sighed, reaching up and giving her mother a kiss on the cheek. "I won't be too late."

"Just have fun, that's all that matters," her mother replied.

The walk to Janice's house was actually fun. Young trick-or-treaters lined the sidewalks, their bags heavy with their candy and their eager faces ready for more houses and more doorbells to ring. They dashed from house to house as tired parents waited on the sidewalks, calling to their children and reminding them to say thank you as the treats were dispersed. Mary grinned, it wasn't that long ago that she was one of the children on the doorstops, bag held out eagerly, looking for her favorite treats. She really wished she was still that age.

She finally reached Janice's house. Janice's dad was a doctor and their house was huge. It was the last house before the forest preserve on Foster Avenue and took up several city lots. The front lawn was decorated with orange pumpkin lights, an animated coffin and trees filled with hanging ghosts. White luminaries lined the sidewalk that led to the front porch and the deck on the side of the house.

With a sigh, Mary started down the sidewalk towards the house. *Maybe I shouldn't be so negative,* she thought. *I might have a good time. I might discover that I do have something in common with these girls. They might decide they like me and want me to hang out with them.*

"She's coming, but her brothers aren't?" the loud voice drifted towards Mary from over the deck rail. "Uh, that's so lame. We should have known she would ruin things."

Mary froze.

"Well, it won't be that bad," another voice said and then there was a pause, followed by a giggle. "Okay, yes, it will."

"Well, we don't have to be nice to her," the first voice laughed. "We can just sit her down in the corner and give her some food. Just like in the lunchroom."

The resounding laughter caused a pit in the middle of Mary's stomach, she felt like she was going to get sick right there on the front lawn. *Oh, yeah, that will make my popularity rise at school,* she thought bitterly. *There goes lunch-corner puke girl.*

Without a second thought, she turned around and walked away, not aware of where she was going or the tears sliding down her cheeks. She had walked for several minutes before she realized she was following a path through the forest preserve. She stopped, wiped the moisture from her face and looked around. The woods were quiet and the air smelled like moist dirt, it seemed to buoy her spirits. She took several deep breaths and reminded herself that she knew what those girls were like, so they just lived up to her expectations.

Now, her only question was what to do with the rest of her evening. She knew if she arrived home early her mother would find out what happened and Margaret Mary Elizabeth O'Reilly would be marching down the street, into Janice's house and demand an apology from all of the girls at the party. That would be mortifying.

Then a thought occurred to her that had her standing up straight. *The Lost Cemetery!*

She'd heard stories about the old cemetery that was hidden in the corner of LaBagh Woods. Her brothers spoke about seeing floating balls of light and hearing voices, but they had always told her she was too young and she would get frightened. She straightened her shoulders and took a deep breath. Well, she wasn't too young tonight. And she would earn a little respect when word got out that instead of going to a stupid party; she spent Halloween in the Lost Cemetery.

She ran down the path towards the wrought iron fence that separated the woods from its neighbor, Montrose Cemetery. The trees on her side of the fence formed a line a few feet away from the fence, creating a canopy of bare branches above and a carpet of dried leaves below. The lights from the cemetery were enough to guide her along the way without tripping.

Finally, she came to the old chain-link fence at the far end of the park. A little way beyond the fence was the bank of the Chicago River and just before the river, in an overgrown clearing was the cemetery. Mary followed the chain-link fence until she found the hole her brothers had told her about. She pushed through it, catching her stockings on a sharp piece of link and snagging them, but continued on into the underbrush.

The woods were darker here and she wished she had thought to bring a flashlight. But there was a full moon and most of the tree branches were bare, so she had enough light to see. The narrow path to the old cemetery was obvious, stamped down vegetation and bare dirt marked the way through the trees and brush.

As she moved forward, her heart beat with anticipation. Would she see floating lights or hear the voices of those who had passed away?

She slowed her pace as she entered the overgrown woods. *Maybe this wasn't such a great idea,* she thought, thinking about all of the scary movies she had ever seen. *This is the kind of place where people are killed and no one ever finds out what happened to them.*

She swallowed nervously and slowly looked around. The forest separated her from everything. She couldn't even hear the traffic from Foster Avenue any more.

Could anyone hear me scream?

A noise ahead of her made her jump and caused her heart to race. Someone was coming. The sound of unruly male laughter drifted down the path and slurred voices accompanied a litany of words she was not allowed to use.

She looked around for a place to hide, but there was nowhere to go. Finally, deciding that her black outfit might hide her if she was closer to the ground, she knelt down and crawled into the brush, away from the path. Branches, thorns and rocks bit through her thin clothes, but she continued on, trying to make as little noise as possible. But when her knee came into sharp contact with a big rock in the ground, she couldn't help it. She cried out.

"What the hell was that?" she heard one of the voices call out.

"A ghost," another voice said, giggling wildly.

"Shut up," the first, angrier voice ordered. "If someone is out here and saw us, we need to make them go away."

Mary curled up next to the stone, that was flat and square, and tried to make herself as small as possible. *Please God*, she prayed, tears squeezing out from eyes clamped shut. *Please help me.*

"Put that flashlight down, you idiot," the angry one yelled. "You want to bring the cops here?"

"Sorry," the other voice replied softly. "I just thought it would help."

"I think the sound came from over here," the angry voice said and Mary felt the brush near her tremble with movement.

Please God, please, she prayed.

Suddenly the forest was filled with sounds, like thousands of cicadas suddenly coming to life.

"Dude, what's that?" the giggler asked.

"Nothing, just bugs," the angry one replied.

But then the sound changed. It was no longer the rustling chirp of the cicada, the sound was now more of a chant. "Leave this place, leave this place, leave this place," in echoing voices that seemed to come from everywhere.

"This is not cool," the voice was now frightened instead of cheerful. "Who's doing this?"

"Leave this place, leave this place, leave this place." The volume increased as if more voices joined the ethereal choir. "Leave this place!"

"Dude, I'm out of here," cried the giggler and Mary could hear his footsteps racing down the path.

"Get back here," called the angry voice, his voice shaking. "I'm not afraid of this!"

Suddenly the woods were silent. As silent as the inside of a tomb. Mary held her breath and grabbed hold of the rock, hugging it for dear life. Then she heard the scream. It seemed to have been pulled out of the depths of the angry man and echoed through the woods.

"No, no, no," he stammered and then she heard his footsteps racing down the path.

She lay still, hugging the stone, her breath coming out in short gasps. She didn't know if she was safe or in even more danger.

"You can come out now," the child's voice was so out of place, that Mary instantly looked up.

A young girl dressed in a pinafore and print dress stood next to Mary. "My father frightened the bad men away," the girl added. "You don't have to be afraid."

"Who are you?" Mary asked, releasing the stone and sitting up.

The child laughed softly and pointed down to the stone Mary had been hugging. "That's me," the little girl replied.

Mary looked down and gasped, realizing for the first time that she had been hugging a gravestone the entire time she'd been hiding. The moon shone down on the granite slab and she read the inscription "Fannie Schweppler, born October, 31, 1840, died April 28, 1848."

She looked back up, but the little girl was no longer there. A chill ran down her spine and she hugged herself for a moment, not trusting her legs to hold her. *I have just seen an actual ghost*, she thought. *Not only that, a ghost family just saved me.*

The fear subsided and gratitude to its place. She put her hand back down on the granite slab. "If there is ever something I can do for you," she whispered. "I will. I owe you."

Finally, she stood, brushed herself off and slowly headed back down the path, listening carefully for any noises that might indicate the two men hadn't been frightened away for good.

She breathed a sigh of relief when she reached Foster Avenue and then jogged the rest of the way home.

The following Monday, the noon bell had rung and Mary stood waiting once again until the crowd cleared out. She walked slowly towards the stairs and met the elderly nun once again.

"Good morning, Sister," she said with a smile.

"How are you today, dear?" the nun asked.

Mary thought about the question for a moment.

How am I, really?

And then she realized she was fine, she was more than fine, she was great.

“I’m great,” she replied confidently. “I’m really great.”

The old nun chuckled and nodded slowly. ““““It’s always a good day when you get to meet a friend. Fannie sends her regards. Have a good lunch, dear.”

“Thank you, Sister,” Mary responded automatically, stepped forward and then stopped.

Fannie!

She turned quickly. “Sister how did you—”

No one was behind her. She ran back into the hall, peeking through the doors in the classrooms closest to where they had been standing. No one was there either. She started to run back down the hall, but stopped and shook her head. She knew the elderly sister would not be in any of the classrooms or anywhere in the school.

“It is always a good day when you *really* get to meet a friend,” she whispered and then shivered a little when she heard the sound of the elderly nun’s laughter echo softly in the hall.

Epilogue

"I never liked that Janice Heppner," Margaret said determinedly, "always just a little too full of herself." She looked over at her daughter. "I wish I had known how those girls treated you."

Mary smiled and rolled her eyes. "Mom, that was over ten years ago, I've recovered, believe me," she said. "Besides, it was one of the coolest nights of my life. I mean, how often does a person actually get to see and talk to a ghost?"

"Well, I don't like the fact that you put your life at risk, going to that cemetery in the middle of the night," Timothy grumbled. "Why if I had known—"

"Sorry, Da, but Ma's given me a free pass on this one," Mary replied. "You can't give me a hard time about it."

"You never told us," Sean said. "You kept that story to yourself all these years. Why?"

Shrugging, Mary studied the flame in the jack o'lantern for a moment and then turned to her brother. "I don't know," she said. "Partly, I guess because I figured I'd get in trouble if I told." She sent an unrepentant grin to her father. "And partly because it was such a cool experience, I didn't know if just telling the story could do it justice."

"Did you ever see the nun again?" Timothy asked.

Mary shook her head. "No, after that I never did," she said. "And I actually missed her. I always felt like she was looking out for me."

"I suppose she knew you didn't need to be watched over any longer," Margaret said. "Or maybe you just didn't need to see her any longer."

"What do you mean, Ma?" Art asked.

"Well, just because we can't see them, doesn't mean that ghosts aren't around," she replied.

Tom chortled, popping some candy into his mouth. "Yeah, like there are ghosts here in this room, right now," he scoffed.

Margaret shrugged. "Could be," she said. "You never know."

"Okay," Tom said, standing up and slowly turning around the room. "If there's a ghost in this house let your presence be known."

Suddenly the candle in the Jack O'Lantern went out and the room was plunged into darkness.

"That was just a weird coincidence, right?" Tom asked, his voice shaking slightly.

Margaret laughed. "Could be," she whispered. "You never know."

The End

Author's notes:

I have always loved ghost stories and I hope you enjoyed these five, created just for the O'Reilly family and shared with you. As in most fiction, some of the information in the stories is based in fact. The old City Cemetery did indeed sit where Lincoln Park now resides and there are still bodies buried underneath the ground. There is a lost cemetery in LaBagh Woods on the northwest side of the city near Montrose Cemetery.

The story about the orphanage came to me when I listened to Kurt Bestor's song, "Prayer Of The Children." It is hauntingly beautiful and was written by Kurt out of frustration over the horrendous civil war and ethnic cleansing taking place in the former country of Yugoslavia. And although those children were topmost in his mind when he wrote it, when we listen to it today we can, unfortunately, see so many more children throughout the world in the same situation as those during the Kosovo War.

It's often hard when we watch our children dressed as ghosts, princesses and superheroes safely walk through local neighborhoods and enjoy trick-or-treating, to remember that other children aren't so lucky. I strongly urge you to take a moment and listen to "Prayer of the Children." And whether your mind is turned to children in your own country who are in harm's way or children throughout the globe that suffer the ravages of war, disease or hunger, I hope that we can all take a moment and, at the very least, say a prayer for the children.

Thank you,

Terri Reid

Book Two

Chapter One

(Twelve years ago)

Rain was coming down in a steady drizzle as it had all night, dampening the costumes of many Trick-or-Treaters but not their spirits as they stoically made their way up to the front porch of the O'Reilly home. Mary opened the door to look at a pair of soggy ghosts and a dampened princess with eye makeup running down her adorable six-year old cheeks. "Trick or treat," they called in unison, holding their treats bags out in front of them.

"Oh, my, you have wonderful costumes," Mary replied with a smile as she placed a handful of candy in each bag. "Did you do well tonight?"

"We got lots," the smiling princess replied. Her front tooth was missing, which turned the last word into a slight lisp that Mary found endearing.

"Lots?" Mary repeated.

The three nodded. "Uh-huh," one of the ghost replied in a slightly more masculine voice. "Lots of kids stayed home 'cause of the rain and people wanted to get rid of their candy."

"Well, it was very wise of you to venture out in the rain," Mary said, wondering why their normally overprotective mother had let them out in such nasty weather. A moment later she had her answer.

Once again, the three nodded. "Yeah, and Mom had to work late, so she won't even know," the tallest of the ghostly pair answered. "Um, what time is it?"

Mary glanced down at her watch. "Almost 8:30."

The three looked at each other, their eyes widening. "We gotta go," the oldest said, picking up his sheet and heading towards the sidewalk. "Bye. Thanks."

"You're welcome," Mary said, biting back a smile as she watched the three run down the sidewalk, their costumes flapping against their legs, their bags held against their chests as they hurried toward their house down the block. "Good luck."

"Are you being a bad influence?" Sean, her older brother, asked as he leaned over her shoulder and watched the three along with her. He reached into the bowl she was holding and pulled out a candy bar.

"No," she said with a grin. "But I could see us doing the exact same thing."

They watched in delight as the kids entered the house just moments before their mother's car pulled into the driveway.

"Do you think they'll get away with it?" she asked her brother.

"Well, if it was me, I'd hightail it upstairs to my bedroom, quickly stash my candy and costume under the bed and then pull on a robe," he said.

"I heard that Sean O'Reilly," his mother called from the living room.

"But I would have never gotten away with it," he said, sending a quick wink towards his sister. "Because Ma would have found us out."

"Because she has eyes in the back of her head," Art O'Reilly, one of the twins, replied.

"Nope, she's psychic," Tom O'Reilly, the other twin, said.

"No, it's because she can read minds," Sean said, as he and Mary joined the rest of the family in the living room.

"Well, if you want to know the truth," Margaret O'Reilly, their mother, said. "It was because you were the worst liars I've ever met."

The adult children were stunned into silence and Timothy O'Reilly, their father, roared with laughter. "And now you've done it, my darling," he said to his wife. "You've given away our greatest secret."

"Well, it's best they know their weaknesses before they go get married and try and lie to a spouse," she said with a chuckle. "Because that would be the end of that."

"But you believe our ghost stories," Mary inserted defiantly.

Her mother smiled at her and nodded. "And that's because they've got truth in them," she said. "Don't they?"

Mary looked around the room at her older siblings and her parents. "All of them?" she asked.

"All of them that will be told around the Jack O'Lantern tonight," her father said, his voice soft. He walked past her, locked the front door and turned off the lights. The front porch was now dark and the only light in the house was from the flickering glow of the Jack O'Lantern's candle placed in the middle of the coffee table. "And now, who's the first to start?"

Chapter Two

"When your father and I were just a young couple and Sean was a wee boy we lived in a small apartment on the north side of the city," Margaret O'Reilly began. "It was a usual Chicago apartment, a long hallway that separated the front living room and a small bedroom from the kitchen, bathroom and another bedroom in the back of the house. We'd set up the front bedroom as a nursery because it got the morning sun and was the warmest room in the house."

And so her story began.

Margaret O'Reilly wiped her hands on her apron and turned off the water in the sink. She had hoped to be able to get the dishes done before Sean woke up, but she could hear his voice calling from the front of the apartment and knew the dishes would have to wait.

Hurrying up the hallway she could hear her son's laughter. He was such a happy boy and, at two years old, more than old enough to be moved out of the crib he was sleeping in and into a bed. But with a tight household budget, the new bed was still a few more months away.

She paused outside the door, with her hand on the doorknob and smiled as she listened to him babble away. It was almost as if he was having a conversation with someone, she thought with a shake of her head. He was quite a talker, her son.

Opening the door, she saw Sean standing in his crib on the side opposite the door. He turned to her and smiled, lifting his arms toward her as he walked over his mattress.

"Momma," he cried, as he hurried. "Momma."

She hurried over and picked him up, kissing him softly on the cheek. "Well, good morning, my big man," she said. "And how did you sleep?"

She turned, walking back towards the door and Sean looked over her shoulder and laughed aloud. Pausing, she turned around to see what caught his fancy, but there was nothing unusual in the room. "What do you see, Sean?" she asked.

He clapped his chubby, little hands together and then looked back towards the closet in the corner of the room. He laughed again, chuckling his deep belly laugh that was generally reserved for when his father was making faces at him. Margaret stared into the corner, lit by the sunlight streaming into the room, and felt a shiver course down her spine.

Taking a deep breath, she shook her head. There was nothing there; she was just spooking herself.

"Okay, well, let's get you some breakfast," she said, holding him closer and turning him away from the corner. "How does oatmeal and brown sugar sound to you?"

"Sugar," Sean repeated with a delighted smile.

She carried him out of the room and closed the door firmly behind her. "I'm just being silly," she said aloud. "There's nothing in there but a child's room."

For the next few days, Margaret felt uneasy about Sean's room. She found herself avoiding the room during the day, keeping Sean with her on the other side of the house, letting him nap on her own bed and play in the living room. When she finally had to put him to bed, she kept the door to his bedroom open, so she could listen for him.

One night, when Timothy had to work late, Margaret was in the kitchen folding laundry when she heard the sound of a child laughing. Glancing up at the clock, she saw it was nearly ten o'clock and wondered what kind of mother allowed her young child to be up at that hour. Worried, she opened the back door of the apartment and stepped out on the porch to see if she could locate the child. But stepping outside she made a realization that had her blood growing cold; there was no noise outside. The laughter she'd heard had come from inside her apartment.

Bolting back into the house she ran up the hallway. Sean's door was closed. She knew she'd kept it open to listen for him. She grabbed the handle and pushed the door open wide, her heart pounding in her chest. Suddenly, she felt foolish. Sean was sound asleep, his fine, blonde hair tossed across his forehead and his little lips drawn upward in a smile. Looking around the room, she could see that everything was in place. His shelves were filled with blocks, cars, trucks and stuffed animals. His favorite books were stacked on his dresser. His teddy bear was in his bed next to him and his favorite toy, a push and spin carousel, was on the floor next to the closet door.

She leaned over the crib, pulled his blanket up and softly kissed his head. "Good night, sweetheart," she whispered. "Pleasant dreams."

Turning, making sure the door was wide open, she returned to the kitchen to finish folding the laundry.

Several hours later, Timothy came home. He entered the front door and then stopped at the front hallway, making sure his gun was stored away high on the shelf and his uniform jacket hung just below it. He paused when he heard some noise coming from his son's room and started to turn in that direction when Margaret called from the kitchen.

"I've got your dinner warming in the oven," she called softly.

He walked down the hall into the kitchen and gave her a quick kiss. "I'll eat in a moment," he said. "I want to go in and see Sean first, while he's awake."

"He's sound asleep," Margaret said. "I checked on him about thirty minutes ago."

"That's funny," Timothy replied. "I'm sure I heard his carousel playing when I walked in the house."

Pushing past her large husband, Margaret ran down the hall to her son's room. Timothy followed closely behind. She stopped at the doorway and swallowed a scream as she stared at the floor in the middle of Sean's room.

"What's wrong?" Timothy asked, coming up behind her.

She couldn't speak, she just pointed.

Sean lay sound asleep, just as he'd been when she'd checked on him. But the little toy, his favorite, was now in the middle of the room and the carousal was still spinning as if someone had just pushed the little plunger down. Then they both heard the sound of a child's soft laughter echoing throughout the room.

Chapter Three

"How long did it take you to move?" Art asked his mother. "And why didn't you leave Sean with the ghost?"

Sean playfully punched his brother in his arm. "Thanks a lot," he quipped.

"It took us about two weeks to move," Margaret said. "But we moved in with a friend during the time it took us to get out of the lease and move to a new place."

Timothy chuckled. "And once your mother sat down with the landlord and let him know exactly how she felt about his haunted apartment, he was only too happy to let us out of the lease," he said.

"So, I've been associating with ghosts since I was little," Sean said, nodding his head slowly. "Okay, that clears somethings up."

"What does that mean?" Mary asked.

"It means I get to tell the next story," he replied. "It was a dark and stormy night." He stopped and laughed. "Actually, it was a beautiful late summer day and I had just arrived on the campus of Notre Dame University."

The main quad at Notre Dame was teaming with new students and Sean was on his way to his new home for the semester, Sorin Hall. He had his arms filled with boxes and had a backpack strung over his shoulders when the building came into view. Stopping in his tracks, his jaw dropped, he just stared.

"Come on," his friend Pete O'Byran said, slapping him on his back to move him forward. "We've got a carload of stuff to carry in."

"Dude, we're going to live in a castle," Sean said, looking at the turrets at each corner. "It's a freaking castle."

"Nope," Pete said. "It's a really old building and it probably has drafts and really old bathrooms."

"How can you say that?" Sean asked. "This place is magical. This place has atmosphere. This place…"

This place has ghosts.

Sean didn't know if he'd heard the words or just felt them. He looked around, but there was no one close except for Pete.

"Did you hear that?" he asked, knowing the answer before he even opened his mouth.

"Hear what?" Pete asked impatiently. "Come on, O'Reilly, stop daydreaming and get moving."

That night after boxes had been emptied, clothes hung up and dinner eaten at the dining hall, Sean found himself wanting to get away from the crowds. Leaving Sorin Hall, he walked towards the main quad. Noises from the dorms and activities on the other side of campus faded away as he walked toward the center of campus and the iconic Washington Hall. Finding himself a bench among the large oak trees spread out among the green, he sat down, placed his elbows on his knees, cradled his head in his hands and sighed. He wondered what his family was having for dinner, which football game Art and Tom were arguing over and what his father had done that day at work.

"It's okay to miss them."

Startled, Sean jumped and turned around to find an elderly priest standing behind him. "I'm so sorry, Father," Sean said. "You startled me."

Chuckling softly, the priest nodded. "Yes, I do have that habit of sneaking up behind the students," he admitted. "Of course, it tends to keep them worried when they're up to no good."

Sean laughed softly. "That's probably a good thing," he admitted. Then he looked around the deserted quad. "Am I allowed here, I mean at night? This is my first day, so I'm not real sure about the rules."

The priest smiled warmly. "Yes, you are allowed here," he said. "Especially when you need a time to be quiet and reflect on your life. That's why I walk the quad."

Impressed with the priest's insight, he nodded. "I didn't think I'd miss them this much," he admitted. "I mean, I'm in college now, I'm not a kid."

The priest's smile widened. "No, you are certainly not a kid," he agreed. "But missing your family has little to do with age or maturity, it has to do with love." He nodded with admiration. "It is a good thing to take the time to think about them and miss them."

Sean felt comfortable chatting with the elderly man. For some reason, he felt as if he could tell him anything. "Duh," he said aloud. "Confession."

The priest shook his head, confused. "I beg your pardon?"

Blushing, Sean rolled his eyes. "I apologize, Father," he said. "I was thinking that for some reason I could tell you anything and you'd understand and then I thought…"

"Ahhh," the priest said with a grin. "Confession." And he laughed. "Yes. Yes, I do see. But, I believe, Sean O'Reilly, that we have something more in common."

"We do? What?" Sean asked, and then he shook his head. "Wait. How do you know my name?"

"I will answer your first question and perhaps that will answer your second," the priest replied, the smile on his face turning thoughtful. "Both you and I, Sean O'Reilly, believe in ghosts."

Then the priest nodded his head and disappeared into the night.

Chapter Four

"Did you ever find out who he was?" Timothy asked.

Sean nodded. "Yeah, as soon as I got back into the dorm," he explained. "I'd been using the door closest to my bedroom and hadn't gone in through the main doors until that night. There was a statue of him in the lobby of Sorin Hall. I had the pleasure of meeting the one and only Father Sorin that night."

"Well, I've a story for you," Timothy said. "But I never found out who the ghost was."

The woman's body had been found beneath the metal staircase that led to the Damen Avenue elevated train stop. Just like the others, she'd been strangled and her hair had been cut off, as if the killer was collecting his own version of scalps. And, unfortunately, he had acquired quite a collection in the six weeks he'd been terrorizing the city.

Timothy O'Reilly had found her body and called it in. He was also the one assigned to go to her family's home and give them the news that the woman who was both mother and wife would never be coming home again. The young widower, with his three children gathered around him, wept openly. Timothy could do nothing for him but place his arm around the young man and let him cry. There were no words of consolation, this man and these children would feel the effects of the killer's action for the rest of their lives. Before leaving the small home, Timothy vowed that he would personally do everything he could to make sure her murderer was caught.

The next day Timothy arrived at the station thirty minutes before his shift and went upstairs to his sergeant's office. He knocked on the door and waited for permission to enter.

"O'Reilly," his sergeant said with a smile. "Good to see you. What's up?"

"I want in on the scalp murders," Timothy replied. "I want to help solve the case."

The sergeant stared at Timothy for a few moments without answering, and then he adjusted the glasses that were resting on his nose and leaned back in his chair. "And this is the same Timothy O'Reilly that's turned down a promotion to detective every time I've offered it to him?" the sergeant asked, his eyebrows raised.

"Aye, it is," Timothy replied. "And I still don't want that blasted job. I just want to help solve this case."

"Why?"

"Why?" Timothy asked. He leaned forward, propping his fingers on the edge of the sergeant's desk and spoke. "I've found three of the women he's murdered. I've had to go to three homes and tell family members that this animal has changed their lives forever," he said slowly and clearly. "I want him caught. I want him tried. I want him locked up forever."

"So, it's personal?" the sergeant asked.

"You tell a four year-old her mommy's not coming home ever again and tell me that it's not personal," he replied.

The sergeant nodded. "Okay, I'm sold," he said. "Let me make a call and I'll let you know."

Timothy stood up and nodded. "Thank you," he said. "I appreciate it."

"Go get ready for your shift and then come back up here before you go out," the sergeant requested.

"Yes sir."

Timothy went down to the locker room to change from his street clothes into his uniform. He walked to the far end of the room where his locker was located, away from most of the younger men in the district. He unbuttoned his shirt and hung it on a hook in the locker, and then he started to pull his t-shirt over his head when he heard someone approaching.

"Hey, old man, you still down here?" one of the younger police officers asked, walking around the wall of lockers.

"Yeah," Timothy said. "What's up?"

"The sergeant wanted me to tell you that your request has been denied," the young cop said. "Says he tried, but no can do. Said it'd be a waste of time coming up to his office. Subject's closed."

Timothy took a deep breath to hold back the anger and nodded to the young man. "Thanks for delivering the message," he said.

"Yeah, thanks for not killing the messenger," the officer replied.

Timothy slammed his locker door and the sound echoed throughout the room. "Dammit," he growled. "Now what?"

Suddenly a file fell from above the lockers and landed at his feet. Bending over, he picked it up. It was a file from the old archives; it was dated ten years ago. Opening the folder he examined it and he shook his head. The victim had been strangled and her hair had been cut off, just like the victims in the current killing spree. He looked at the file in his hand and then up to the top of the lockers. How the hell had this file made its way to the locker rooms? Well, he wasn't going to look a gift horse in the mouth. Now all he had to do was check the archive for any other files like this one.

The archives were in the lowest level of the building in cardboard file boxes on a series of steel shelves. Opening the door, he flipped on the light and stared at the hundreds of boxes before him. How in the world was he ever going to find the right files?

He looked at the date on the file he carried. He could start with the date, he thought. At least that would get him in the vicinity. He started to walk towards the back of the large room when he heard a noise coming from the side of the room. It sounded like a box had been moved. He turned and noticed one of the boxes was out of alignment with the others. Could that have been the box that this file had been taken from?

He hurried over and examined the box. Yes, it had the same dates. Lifting the cover, he flipped through the files and found three more folders with the same MO from a crime that was never solved. "These are good," he said softly. "But why wasn't this cased solved? There was enough evidence."

Suddenly a box across the room slipped from the top shelf of a shelving unit and crashed to the floor. Timothy looked around. Nothing could have caused the box to move. His heart pounded in his chest. Nothing human.

The radio on his belt squeaked and Timothy jumped. "O'Reilly," the voice came over the speaker and he recognized it as his sergeant. "Where the hell are you?"

Timothy picked up the radio and pressed the button. "I'm doing some paperwork," he said. "What's up?"

"I want you up in my office, pronto," the sergeant replied.

"Yes, sir," Timothy answered.

"Don't go."

Timothy froze. That wasn't just a box moving or a file falling, that was a voice.

"What did you say?" he asked, his voice a squeaking whisper.

"Don't go. They'll kill you."

Timothy shook his head. "No, they won't do that," he said. "The sarge is a good guy."

"They killed me," the voice replied.

"What?" Timothy asked, too confused to be frightened.

His heart beat even faster when he noticed a folder slowly working its way out from between the other folders crammed into the box, as if an invisible hand was pulling it out. It slid out of the box and floated through the air until it was hanging directly in front of Timothy. He took a deep breath and then grabbed it. The outside labeled the folder as classified. "I can't look at this," Timothy said.

"You must."

Taking a deep breath, Timothy opened the file and looked inside. There was a signed confession to the scalp murders from the former mayor's nephew dated from ten years ago. Timothy shook his head. The former mayor's nephew had just been named to a position in City Hall. He'd never gone to jail. Never been prosecuted.

"Take it to Judge Tomlinson," the voice whispered. *"Now. Tonight."*

"How about Judge Callahan?" Timothy asked, naming another judge he'd worked with.

He thought he heard an ironic chuckle and then the voice replied. *"No. Judge Tomlinson. Now."*

Timothy started toward the door when he heard noise coming from the other side. "Damn," he whispered. "The jigs up."

"Not yet."

Suddenly the lights went out and Timothy was plunged into darkness. He heard startled voices on the other side of the door as they searched for light. But he knew it wouldn't be too long before they'd turned on their flashlights and made their way inside.

"This way."

Timothy looked around and saw the faintly illuminated figure of a man. *"Follow me."*

He was led to a small window back behind the shelves and was able to crawl out. Once he reached the outside, he turned back to thank whoever it was who'd helped him. But all he saw was darkness.

He drove his own car to the judge's house and presented her with the files. Within a few hours, several high-ranking police officials, including his own sergeant, were arrested for conspiracy. And Timothy never heard the voice again.

Chapter Five

"Do you have any idea who he might have been?" Art asked his father.

Timothy shook his head. "I have my own theories," he said. "But nothing I could ever prove."

Margaret reached over and took his hand in hers. "Whoever he was, I'll be eternally grateful," she said. "And I hope one day he finds peace. And I hope they find out who killed him."

"I'm sure they will," Timothy said. "When it's the right time."

"Speaking of the right time," Art inserted. "How long is the statute of limitations on not telling your parents the truth?"

Margaret glanced over at him and shook her head. "There is no statute of limitations on that." Then she smiled. "But if we're going to get a good story from it, we'll grant you clemency."

"Well, I hope it's a good story," Art said. "Sure scared the heck out of me. It happened back in high school when I was trying out for the basketball team…"

Several dozen young men sat in the bleachers, wearing their school issued gym clothes, waiting nervously for their name to be called by the coach. Once on the polished wood gym floor they would be put through their paces; doing lay-ups, dribbling the ball and making shots from the free-throw line. Then the coach would have them play a one-on-one game with one of the members of the Varsity team. It was generally a humiliating experience for the student trying out, one that Art O'Reilly wasn't looking forward to.

Being an O'Reilly was a blessing and a curse, especially when your older brother was a school icon. Sean had played football, basketball, baseball and excelled in each. His grades were good, he had never done anything dorky and despite it all, he was actually a nice guy. Coming up behind his brother in school, the twins were very often compared to their older brother's accomplishments. He could still remember a woodshop class where the teacher held up his project, smiled encouragingly and said, "This is good, O'Reilly, pretty good. But you should see what your brother did." Then, to Art's mortification, the teacher went to his backroom and pulled out the three year-old project his brother had done. "I saved this," the teacher said in a reverential voice, displaying it to the entire class. "Because no other student has ever come this close to fulfilling the artistic aspect of this project."

Art had wanted to crawl under his desk. And, now, here he was again. Sean had been a point guard, arguably the most important position on the team, and he had been great. The coach, seeing the last name O'Reilly, was probably expecting more of the same. But Art didn't want to be a superstar. Didn't think he could. He just wanted to play the game.

The coach called name after name on the roster and the minutes clicked by on the clock. Art had purposely put his name on the very bottom. He didn't want an audience to experience his probable humiliation. He glanced over at the locker room. Maybe he should just hide out, not be there when the coach called his name. The more he thought about it, the better the idea seemed. So, sliding between the bleacher seats, he dropped down to the floor and scurried out of the room.

The locker room was deserted, but Art could hear voices coming close. Probably the last few guys who'd been creamed by the Varsity players. He certainly didn't want to be found hiding. Looking around he saw a door, his only choice for escape. He hurried over and turned the doorknob. Luck was finally with him, it was unlocked. Slipping inside, he pulled the door closed behind him.

The room was about the size of a small classroom and as tall as the gymnasium. About ten feet up there was a small, opaque window that, in the afternoon sun, gave the room a murky glow. The room was filled with equipment that was either outdated, or used at different times of the year. One corner held gymnastics equipment, another a pile of cotton mats about three feet high and boxes of basketballs, volleyballs and softballs were scattered all around the rest of the room. Walking over to the mats, he jumped up on them and laid down. He might as well get comfortable while he waited.

Art got too comfortable and a few hours later woke up to a darkened room with only a dim glow from an outside streetlamp filtering through the window.

"You okay?"

Art jumped at the sound of the voice and turned to see another young man standing on the other side of the room. He breathed a sigh of relief and smiled. "Yeah, I'm good," he replied. "I guess I just fell asleep."

"Why are you in here?" the young man asked.

Art studied the boy for a moment. He didn't look familiar and was dressed in gym clothes that looked a little strange. Maybe he was new to the school. "I'm kind of hiding out," he admitted. "My brother was like this huge jock a couple of years ago and I'm not as good as he was. So, instead of being publically humiliated, I decided to check out this room."

The young man laughed. "Come on, you can't be that bad," he said.

Art nodded. "Oh yes, I can," he said with a smirk. "I'm Art. Art O'Reilly, by the way."

"Bobby," the young man said. "Bobby Forester. Good to meet you."

Tossing a basketball at him, Bobby angled his head towards the door. "Come on, there's no one out there now," he said. "Why don't you show me what you can do?"

They walked out into the gym and Art went to flip on the lights when Bobby stopped him. "Better keep those off so we don't alert the custodian and get in trouble," he said. "Besides, there's enough light in here to shoot."

Art looked around. With the emergency lights glowing high in the ceiling and the glow of the streetlights through the window, there was certainly enough light to shoot a few baskets. "Sounds good to me," he agreed and slowly dribbled the ball across the floor to the free throw line. "I probably should always play basketball in the dark."

Bobby chuckled. "Okay, let's see your free throw."

Art bounced the ball a couple of times, lifted it, balanced it with one hand and pushed it off with the other. The ball sailed through the air, bounced against the rim and sailed back towards Art. "That was my boomerang shot," Art said, shaking his head with disgust. "I have a bunch just like that."

"Hey, great shot," Bobby said, coming up next to Art. "But this time, don't flex your wrist as much."

"What do you mean?" Art asked.

Bobby demonstrated the move, the ball sailed up and through the basket, no rim, only net.

"That was awesome," Art said with a sigh.

"You do it now," Bobby said.

Art shook his head. "I'll try and I hope you're not too disappointed."

He followed Bobby's advice and found, more often than not, he was able to make the same kind of shot Bobby had made. "This is amazing," he said with a wide smile.

"Come on," Bobby said. "Let me show you a few more moves."

They played for several hours until Art looked up at the caged clock on the wall and saw that it was after ten o'clock. "My mom is going to kill me," he said to Bobby. "I've got to go. But thanks, thanks so much. You changed my life."

Bobby smiled at Art. "Hey, it only took a couple of pointers," he said. "You're a natural."

"Are you trying out tomorrow?" Art asked. "You ought to. You are amazing."

Bobby nodded. "I'll think about it," he said. "And thanks for practicing with me tonight. It's been a long time since I've had so much fun."

Art grabbed his jacket and his backpack. "Are you coming?"

Bobby shook his head. "No, I'm going to practice for a little while longer."

"Okay. Thanks again," Art said. "See you tomorrow."

Art jogged home and entered through the basement, finding his twin, Tom, sitting in the family room watching television. "Where have you been?" Tom asked. "I've been both you and me all night, and let me tell you, it's exhausting."

"Hey, thanks," Art replied. "I was at the school. Some guy I met gave me some great tips for basketball. I might actually make the team."

"Well, congrats," Tom said. "By the way, I ate your portion of dessert too."

"Oh, thanks," Art replied sarcastically. "Thanks a lot."

The next afternoon, Art was actually eager for the coach to call his name. When he finally got his turn he was able to implement all of the tricks Bobby had taught him and impress the coach. Finally, when it was time to meet the Varsity player, Art used a couple of the moves Bobby had showed him the night before and was able to get around the player and actually even make a shot.

Art was amazed when the coach stood up and applauded. "That was great, O'Reilly," he said. "I haven't seen moves like that since…"

"My brother, Sean, right?" Art asked, his happiness fading.

"No, I was going to say since Forester," the coach replied.

"Forester?" Art asked. "Bobby Forester?"

The coach smiled. "Yeah, he was a great kid," he said. "Could have gone pro."

A chill ran up Art's spine. "What happened to Bobby?" he asked.

"He was killed in a car accident coming to the last game of the season," the coach explained. "Some drunk driver ran a red light. But, you know, sometimes I feel like he's still here with us."

"Yeah," Art replied slowly. "I feel that way too."

Chapter Six

Margaret turned to Tom after Art had finished his story. "So, you were both you and your brother for the whole night?" she asked, her eyebrows raising. "And just how many times have you done that?"

Tom grinned. "Oh, just once or twice, Ma," he replied. "Just once or twice."

"And what would have happened if your brother had been in trouble and we didn't know it because you were pretending to be him?" she asked.

"I would have known Ma," he replied easily. "I always know when Art's in trouble. It's a twin thing."

"A twin thing?" she asked skeptically.

He paused for a moment and then met her eyes. "Or maybe a triplet thing?" he asked softly.

Margaret gasped. "How did you know?"

"I guess it's time to tell my story," he replied.

It was a hot summer night. The cicadas were buzzing in the trees outside their house. The windows were open with box fans whirring at top speed, trying to move the hot and humid air throughout the house.

Tom O'Reilly lay on the bottom level of the bunkbed he shared with his twin brother, Art. The heat was making it hard for him to sleep and, because Tom was the younger twin, Art got the top bunk where the breeze was better. At eight years-old, Tom's outstretched legs could just reach the net of wired squares that held the mattress up above him and if he curled his toes through the metal, he could jostle the mattress and kick his brother. He thumped at the mattress once. "Art are you awake?" he called. No response. He thumped it again. Nothing.

With a frustrated sigh, Tom grabbed his pillow and headed out of the room. Maybe sleeping on the back porch would be cooler.

Standing in the darkened hallway outside his bedroom, Tom listened for a moment to the unique sounds of his house at night. He heard the soft whirr of the box fans, the low rumble of the refrigerator, the annoying drip in the upstairs bathroom sink and the rhythmic growl of his dad's snoring. Tiptoeing down the stairs, he reached the living room and looked around. The soft light from the streetlamps outside cast weird shadows inside the house. Everything looked a little bit different without the light on.

He crept down the hall to the kitchen. The cat clock on the wall, its tail moving in sync with its eyes, freaked him out during the day. He purposely turned away from the soft tick-tock, avoiding its face in the shadowy light. The door to the screened-in back porch was open, another box fan placed in the doorway, directing air from the outside into the house. Tom stepped around the fan and walked over to the canvas-covered green-striped davenport against the wall.

Throwing his pillow down, he climbed onto the couch and lay down, feeling a cooling breeze wash over his body. He stretched and smiled, finally he was going to be able to sleep. He started to close his eyes when a movement caught his attention next to the door. He turned and saw Art standing on the other side of the fan.

"Hey, I thought you were asleep," he said. "Why didn't you answer me?"

Art didn't say a word.

"What?" Tom asked. "You want to sleep here too?"

Art still didn't answer.

Frustrated and tired, Tom turned away from his brother. "Fine, do what you want to do. I'm going to sleep."

Tom woke up several hours feeling disoriented. It took him a few moments to realize he was on the porch and then he remembered what he'd done. He rolled over, towards the kitchen door and was surprised to see Art still standing there watching him.

"Why are you standing there?" he asked sleepily.

"You need to come upstairs," his brother said.

"Why? It's hot up there," Tom argued.

"You need to come upstairs now," his brother replied urgently.

"But…" Tom stopped. Art wasn't standing there anymore. Had he already gone upstairs without him?

He punched his pillow, but then slid off the davenport and hurried through the house back to the staircase. When he got there, he noticed a funny smell. As he climbed the stairs, the smell got stronger, like a campfire, but a stinky one.

"Art," he whispered. "Art where are you?"

He reached the top stair and noticed the smoke. He dashed to his room and touched the doorknob, jerking back and shouting in pain. The doorknob was hot.

"Art," he screamed. "Art are you in there?"

"What's going on?" his father called from the end of the hall.

"There's a fire and Art's in there," Tom screamed.

Timothy ran down the hall and threw his weight against the door. It crashed open and Tom could see a fire blazing in the corner of his room. Timothy ran over to the bunkbed, grabbed Art from the top bunk and ran from the room.

"What's wrong with him?" Tom pleaded, his heart filling with dread as he watched his father carry the lifeless body of his brother into his parent's bedroom. "He was just awake."

"Sean, take the fire extinguisher and spray the fire," Timothy ordered his oldest son. "Margaret call the fire department and tell them we need an ambulance."

Tom hurried over to his brother's side, holding Art's inert hand in his own. "He was just awake," he insisted through his tears. "He wanted me to come upstairs, but he was just awake."

Timothy leaned over his son and performed CPR, breathing into his son's mouth, massaging his chest and then listening for a response. "Come on Art," he pleaded. "Come back to us."

"Art, you gotta come back," Tom said. "I need you."

A moment later, Art coughed and Tom and Timothy met each other's tear filled eyes. "He's going to be fine," Timothy whispered in a broken voice. "He's going to be fine."

Several hours later, the house was quiet again. The fire department had been to the house and claimed faulty wiring in the box fan had caused the fire. The fumes from the burning plastic had nearly suffocated Art and if they hadn't found him when they did...

They had called Tom a hero, but, as he lay back on the davenport in the screened-in porch he didn't feel like one. His mother and father were at the hospital with Art. Sean was sleeping on the couch in the living room and he was back where everything had started.

"But Art was awake," he whispered. "I saw him."

"No, you saw me."

Tom looked over and saw Art standing next to the kitchen door. He felt a chill run down his spine. "Are you Art?" he stuttered softly.

The boy shook his head. "No, I'm the other one," he said softly.

"The other one?" Tom asked, his voice shaking. "What other one?"

"The one that died," the boy replied and then he faded away.

Chapter Seven

Margaret O'Reilly was weeping softly into a tissue. "I had no idea," she cried. "The three of you were so little when you were born and little Gregory only lived for a few hours."

"Yes, he told me," Tom said.

"Told you?" Margaret asked.

"He came back a couple of times," he replied with an easy shrug. "I thought it was cool to have an angel brother. And it was neat because he looked just like Art and me. It was like he was growing up with us. He checks in now and then to see how his family is doing."

Margaret reached over and clasped her son's hand. "Thank you," she said. "A mother's heart always yearns for her lost babies. It's so wonderful to know he's fine."

"And I suppose you never know who's sharing your house with you," Tom said with a wink.

"Which opens the door to my story," Mary said. "The part about not knowing who is sharing your house with you."

Pumpkin was very large, very spoiled and very determined to get his own way. Pumpkin was the O'Reilly's marmalade cat. Pumpkin chose the O'Reilly family when Mary was three years old. He wandered into the yard, climbed up on one of the chairs Mary had arranged for her tea party and daintily lapped away at the cream-heavy tea. Mary was delighted.

Because Pumpkin had first come to Mary, the little girl had decided that he must be her cat. So poor Pumpkin had been subject to all sorts of indignities the average cat would not have put up with. Quite often, he was adorned with bonnets, ribbons, doll dresses and an occasional barrette encircled a clump of his orange hair. He went for rides in doll carriages, sipped tea from a platter and listened to the endless chatter of an excited toddler. Pumpkin was a good sport and a true gentleman. Not once did he extend his sharp claws and exact revenge for the humiliations he encountered. He took it all in stride.

At night, once Mary had gone to bed, Pumpkin would come downstairs and curl himself up on the back of the couch, closest to the fireplace. He would purr happily, enjoying the warmth from the fire and the soft, calming conversation of the two adults who shared his room.

He didn't mind the adults at all. After all, the one called Ma would feed him every day and made sure his water bowl was clean and filled. And the one called Da would scratch him in the most delicious ways.

However, once they turned off the lights and locked the doors, Pumpkin knew it was time for him to assume his nighttime post. With his tail waving tall in the air, Pumpkin would march upstairs and over to Mary's bedroom door. With agility Houdini would have admired, he stood on his back legs, reached up to the doorknob and gave it a slight twist. The door slowly opened several inches under his weight, enough for him to slip through and head to his final destination, Mary's bed. Hopping up on the bed, he walked around until he found his favorite spot, nestled against her back. With a satisfied sigh, he would close his eyes and fall asleep.

Mary and Pumpkin shared many delightful days, but as the years passed and the toddler grew into a child, Pumpkin found himself spending more time watching out the window for his favorite person to come home. He spent most of his days helping out in the kitchen, making sure Ma knew that she was loved by intertwining himself between her legs. Especially when she was doing some mundane task like carrying baskets of laundry or mopping the floor. He could tell she appreciated his attention and would generally ignore any less than polite comments she offered in his direction.

When Mary came home, he would follow her upstairs and sit on the desk as she worked on her homework. And every night, like clockwork, he would open her door, lay down next to her and go to sleep.

More years passed and Pumpkin got to be an old man. The stairs were harder to climb, Mary had to reach down and lift him up on the bed, and he was often very tired. Worried about her friend, Mary would make sure she took the time to pet him and let him know how much she loved him.

One night, after Mary had gone to bed, Pumpkin lay on the couch soaking in the warmth of the fire. His breathing was shallow and he was feeling so very tired. He knew he needed to get up soon, go up to Mary's room for the night, but he couldn't find the energy. Finally, he just closed his eyes.

Ma came into the room and found Pumpkin on the back of the couch. His old body was still and he was no longer breathing. With tears in her eyes, she cradled the cat to her chest and pressed a kiss on his forehead. "Goodbye, my sweet friend," she whispered hoarsely. "You will be missed."

Later than night, Mary woke to the sound of her door opening. Half-asleep, she smiled, and started to slip out of the covers to help Pumpkin into the bed. But before her feet touched the floor in the dark room, she felt the familiar weight of Pumpkin on the mattress. "Good boy," she said, sleepily, laying her head back down on her pillow. "You did it all by yourself."

She felt him walk across the bed, nestle down next to her and heard his contented purring. Pumpkin was right where he belonged.

Chapter Eight

Once again, Margaret O'Reilly was wiping her eyes with a tissue. "I loved that cat," she sniffed.

"You called him a bothersome creature," Timothy reminded her.

"I call you a bothersome creature too," she replied. "And I still love you."

Timothy chuckled. "Aye, that's true," he said. Standing he leaned over and blew out the Jack O'Lantern. "Another Halloween has passed and another great night of storytelling has occurred. And now, I believe, it's time for all of you to go to bed."

Mary gave each of her parents a hug and then climbed the stairs to her bedroom. She quickly washed up, changed into her pajamas and then climbed into bed. She leaned over and clicked off the light on her nightstand, plunging her bedroom into darkness and then she waited. A few minutes later, she heard the sound of her doorknob moving and the door opening slightly. Her head snuggled into the pillow she held her breath until she felt the familiar feline weight on her bed. A moment later, she felt pressure against the small of her back and heard the familiar soft strains of a contented purr.

"Good night, Pumpkin," she whispered, feeling safe and protected. "Sweet dreams."

Author's notes:

I have always loved ghost stories and I hope you enjoyed these six, created just for the O'Reilly family and shared with you. I have a Scottish Prayer hanging in my office that reads, "From Ghoulies and Ghosties and Long-Legged Beasties and Things that go Bump in the Night, Dear Lord, Protect Us."

I hope your Halloween is filled with treats and not tricks, princesses, superheroes and minions, not ghoulies and ghosties, and wonderful memories for you and your family.

Happy Halloween,

Terri Reid

Book Three

Chapter One

(Thirteen years ago)

Margaret O'Reilly stood at the front window peering out into the night. The Jack O'Lanterns on the front porch had been extinguished and the large steel candy bowl had been retrieved. There were rules now for trick or treating; only store-purchased treats and curfews to get children inside before it got too late. She certainly did not want to be accused of tempting the children to stay out past the allotted time. And it was past the allotted time, quite a ways past the allotted time.

"He's fine, Margaret," her husband, Timothy, said softly, coming up behind his wife and laying a hand on her shoulder. "You mustn't worry."

She sighed. "I know I shouldn't, but I can't help it," she whispered back. "He's always on time for our stories."

"He probably got caught up at work," Timothy insisted. "He's safe. You'd know if he wasn't."

She nodded, but kept her vigil at the window. "I'll feel better when I see him pull up at the curb," she said.

Mary walked into the room, a large glass of Diet Pepsi in one hand and a chocolate candy bar in the other. "I just got a text from Sean," she announced. "He's on his way."

Margaret felt the relief wash over her like an ocean wave. Timothy squeezed her shoulder softly. "There you go," he said. "Now come and relax for a few minutes, so he doesn't see the worry in your eyes."

She stepped back, let the curtain fall back in place and faced her husband. "You couldn't have all been something safe, like bakers," she quipped. "No, you had to all up and become police officers."

"Bakers, Ma?" Art replied. "We'd all weigh 300 pounds and die of heart attacks."

"Or get our arms pulled off by those giant mixing machines," Tom added.

"Or eat raw cookie dough and die an awful death," Mary teased.

Margaret grinned and shook her head. "Enough, the three of you have no respect for your mother," she complained mildly.

Art walked over and enfolded his petite mother in his arms. "We have respect, fear and love," he said softly. "Mostly love. But we don't want you to worry."

She brushed a hand quickly over her moist eyes. "It's a mother's prerogative to worry," she said, placing a kiss on her son's cheek. "But thank you for the hug."

Everyone paused and looked towards the door when they heard a car pulling up at the curb.

"That's got to be Sean," Mary said, walking toward the door. "About time."

She opened the door just as Sean dashed up the steps. "Hey, sorry I'm late," he said breathlessly, grabbing a candy bar out of the stainless steel bowl sitting on the entryway table. "But I had to stay late to hear the rest of the story."

"What?" Art asked. "You stayed late because of a story? On Halloween night?"

"Not just any story," Sean said, moving over to the front room and sitting in a chair. "A ghost story." He looked at them and grinned. "A really great ghost story."

Timothy turned off the lights in the room, so the only illumination was the flickering glow of the Jack O'Lantern on the coffee table. "Well, then, sit yourselves down," he said. "And let's get this evening going. Sean, it looks like you'll be first."

Sean nodded. "Great! This is so cool," he began. "So, my part of the story started this evening around seven, but the story really started about a month ago when Martin and Kelly Medford, a brother and sister, were out late one night."

Chapter Two

"We should probably go home," Kelly Medford said to her twin brother, Martin, as they drove away from the high school stadium. "It's late and we both have to work tomorrow."

Martin glanced over at his sister, then shook his head. "There's a party at Joe's," he argued. "We don't have to stay real late, but we need to at least show up."

"Joe's is all the way on the other side of town," Kelly replied. "It's too close to the city. Mom won't like us going into the city."

Martin rolled his eyes. "Who says Mom has to know?"

Kelly sighed and flopped back in her seat. "Fine, we can go," she agreed. "But we can't stay long."

They arrived at Joe's house about twenty minutes later and, before long, they had forgotten about their mutual promise to leave early. When Kelly finally took the time to glance at her phone, she was shocked at the time. "Crap," she exclaimed, looking around the house for her brother. "It's after two."

She finally found him engaged in an argument about the Chicago Bears offensive line with a bunch of the football players. “Martin,” she said, interrupting him. “It’s past two. We are so dead.”

In disbelief, Martin pulled his own phone out and looked. “We’ve got to go,” he said to his friends and they both hurried out of the house.

“I thought you were going to watch the time,” he accused as they walked down the dark street toward their car.

“I never said that,” Kelly replied. “You’re the one who wanted to go.”

“Don’t give me that,” he argued back. “You were having just as much fun as…” Martin paused and then exhaled loudly. “Great.”

Kelly looked over at her brother. “What?”

Then she saw the officer standing next to their car. “What did you do?” she whispered to her brother as they walked slowly toward the officer.

“I might have parked a little close to a fire hydrant,” he whispered back.

“You are such an idiot,” she whispered fiercely. “Now we really are dead.”

They walked up to the car, the officer was standing on the other side, in the road. “This your car?” he asked.

The two nodded. "Yeah," Martin said, his voice low. "It's ours."

"Aren't you a little young to be out so late?" the officer asked.

"We were at our friend's house up the block and we lost track of time," Kelly inserted. "We're really sorry."

The policeman paused for a moment, looking at the teens before pulling out a notebook. "I won't give you a ticket for breaking curfew," he said. "But I've got to give you one for parking. If there had been a fire, your car would have blocked access to the hydrant. You need to be more aware of where you park."

"Yes sir," Martin replied. "You're right. I'm sorry."

"Can I have your driver's license please?"

Martin handed over his license and they stood in the cold night air, waiting while the officer transferred the information from the license to the ticket. Finally, he ripped the ticket from the pad and handed it and the license back to Martin. "You have a month to pay the ticket," he said. "It shouldn't go on your permanent record unless you get another ticket in the next thirty days."

"We won't," Kelly assured him. "We'll be very safe."

He nodded and his lips turned up into a half-smile. "See that you are," he replied, then he turned away and walked back down the street.

Kelly and Martin lost no time in getting into their car and starting the drive home.

"Remember, no speeding," she cautioned her brother.

He nodded. "Yeah, I know," he said. "For all of our luck, he's following us making sure I don't make another mistake."

"We are so dead," Kelly said. "When Mom and Dad find out about the ticket…"

"They won't find out," Martin said. "We'll just pay it ourselves."

"Do you know how much it is?" Kelly asked. "One hundred bucks."

"We'll have to work overtime and save our spending money," he replied. "We can't let them know."

They drove in silence for a few minutes, each lost in their own thoughts.

"Hey, Kel," Martin finally said.

"Yeah?"

"You know, that policeman," he continued hesitantly. "Did he..."

"Did he what?"

"Did he kind of give you the willies?

"What?" she asked, surprised.

"Did he kind of freak you out?" Martin asked.

She shook her head. "No. I don't think so," she answered. "I was just freaked out by getting a ticket."

Martin nodded. "Yeah, you're probably right."

Over the next few weeks, the two teens worked overtime and skipped lunches in order to save up the money to pay their ticket. Finally, nearly one month from the day they received their ticket, they went to the Police Station near Joe's house to pay their fine.

They had decided to pay their fine a little early, so they could go on Halloween night, using the evening's activities as an excuse to be gone for so long. They entered the station at about seven and looked around the lobby.

"Hey, can I help you?" Sean O'Reilly asked the two teens who looked lost and a little overwhelmed.

"Uh, we need to pay for a parking ticket," Martin said.

"You know that you can do that online," Sean offered.

"Yeah, we know," Kelly said. "But…"

"You don't want your parents to find out, right?" Sean asked with a grin.

"Exactly," Martin said with a sigh of relief.

"Okay, come on over here," Sean said. "I'm sure Officer Kasniewski can help you."

Sean walked the teens over to see Zoe Kasniewski, the desk officer for the day. "Hey, Kaz, can you help these two get this ticket paid so they can enjoy their Halloween?" he asked.

"Sure," she replied, reaching out from behind the bullet-proof window. "Let me see the ticket."

Martin handed her the ticket and she glanced over it. Rolling her eyes, she shook her head. "No, sorry, I'm afraid I can't help you," she said.

"What?" Sean, Martin and Kelly asked in concert.

Kaz looked at the teens. "Look, you don't have to pay it," she said. "You're good."

"Wait. Why not?" Martin asked. "I don't want this to go on my permanent record."

"You don't have to pay it because this isn't a real ticket," Kaz replied.

"We saw the cop who gave it to us," Kelly insisted. "He was real."

"What did he look like?" Kaz asked.

"He was tall," Martin said. "Taller than me. Like six two."

Kelly nodded. "It was dark outside, but I think he had brown hair, cut short, and brown eyes. And his tag said "Werner" just like the signature on the ticket."

Sean flinched and glanced at Kaz who caught his glance and nodded slowly. "Yeah," Kaz said to the teens. "We get a couple of tickets a year from this guy. He used to be a cop, but he isn't anymore. So, you're good. Believe me."

"We don't have to pay?" Martin asked.

"No, you're good," Kaz insisted. "Happy Halloween."

Sean waited until the teens had walked out of the lobby before he leaned over towards Kaz. "Werner?" he asked.

She nodded. "I get a couple every year."

"Really? Werner?" he repeated.

She smiled. "Weird right?" she asked. "But I guess you can't keep a good cop down."

"You should have told them," Sean said. "You should have told them the truth."

Kaz smiled. "Yeah, especially tonight," she replied. "Hey kids, just wanted you to know that you received a parking ticket from a cop whose been dead for six years."

Sean winked at her. "Yeah, Happy Halloween."

Chapter Three

"Seriously?" Tom asked when Sean had finished. "It was Werner?"

Sean nodded. "Kaz swears she sees them at least a couple of times a year," he replied, picking up a handful of candy corn and popping it into his mouth. "Weird, right?"

"Well, not so weird," Timothy said with an exaggerated sigh. "Not when you've seen all I've seen in my day."

His children smiled at each other as they readied themselves for their father's tale.

"Back in the day when you had to walk uphill both ways to go to school," Art said.

"Enough sass out of you, young man," Timothy replied with a smile. "I'll share a story that will have you looking over your shoulder at night. Still sends shivers down me own spine and it happened more than thirty years ago."

Timothy O'Reilly was a young police officer with the Chicago Police Department. He was well-liked and, more importantly, well-respected by his peers and his superiors. Arriving at the station early one morning, he was summoned to his Chief's office. He had to admit, he was feeling a little bit of trepidation as he climbed the steps from the locker room in the basement to the second floor where the Chief's office stood. He wondered what he could have possibly done wrong and mentally reviewed the last couple days on the job. Nothing was wrong as far as he could remember.

Finally, he arrived at the office door and knocked.

"Enter," came the command from the inside.

Timothy opened the door and slipped in. "Officer O'Reilly," he announced. "You sent for me, sir?"

The Chief looked up from his paperwork and studied Timothy for a long moment. "Yes, I did," he finally said. "I need you for a special assignment today."

Timothy nodded. "Of course," he replied.

"I need you to take this evidence parcel to Champaign, IL, to their courthouse," he said, pointing to a small cardboard box on the edge of his desk. Then he picked up a piece of paper on his desk and held it out for Timothy. "Here's the directions to the courthouse and the name of the person you need to give it to."

Timothy scanned the paper and then looked up.

"Any questions?" the Chief asked.

Shaking his head, Timothy tucked the folded paper in his pocket. "No sir," he answered.

"Good," the Chief replied. "They'll have a car waiting for you at the garage downstairs. Just drive there and drive back."

"Yes sir," Timothy said, picking up the parcel from the corner of the desk.

The squad car was waiting for him downstairs. "Hey, O'Reilly," the head mechanic said as he handed him the keys. "We've been having some problems with this one, but the Chief didn't give us enough notice to get you one of the newer squads."

"What kind of problems?" Timothy asked.

The mechanic shrugged. "It just kind of quits on you for no reason," he said.

"Well, that could be a problem on the highway," Timothy said.

"Yeah, exactly," the mechanic replied. "So, where you can, take the backroads and if you get into any problems, call me and I'll send a wrecker out to rescue you."

The mechanic gave Timothy a slightly greasy slip of paper with a phone number scribbled on it.

Shoving it in his pocket, Timothy nodded. “I’m hoping I don’t have to use it,” he said.

“Yeah, me too,” the mechanic agreed.

Timothy decided to take a risk and he hopped on the expressway out of the city, headed south toward Champaign. It was a late summer day and, once he’d driven beyond the city limits, cornfields with their crops as tall as a man were already beginning to brown in the fields on either side of Highway 57. The drive was peaceful and the squad car was operating well. In no time at all, he arrived at the courthouse and delivered his package to the clerk.

He’d made good time, so he allowed himself a few minutes for a quick lunchbreak at Ott’s Drive-In about twenty miles north of Champaign in Rantoul. After ordering a burger, fries and chocolate shake, he pushed the seat back in the squad car and enjoyed his meal. The day couldn’t have gone any better, he decided. He’d have to take Margaret down to Champaign sometime, he was sure she’d enjoy the drive.

When he’d finished the last fry and sipped the final bit of shake, he stuffed the wrappers in the bag and turned on the squad car. But it didn’t start. He tried again, but it didn’t react. He really didn’t like the idea of calling a wrecker to come to a Drive-In. Not that he’d done anything wrong by taking a lunch break, but he could already imagine the jabs he’d get at the station.

Reaching down, he unlatched the hood. He didn't know a thing about cars, but maybe luck would be smiling down on him and he'd see something obvious. Once under the hood, he poked and prodded at things underneath, hoping something would help get his car started. With his fingers crossed for good luck, he went back to the driver's seat and tried again. It started immediately.

Taking no chance, he kept the car running while he got out, threw away his garbage and closed the hood. He looked down at the map alongside him. The main highway was several miles to the west, but there was a smaller country road, that led up into Chicago that just about paralleled the road. Just in case, he decided on the back road.

Once again, the drive was beautiful. Timothy got up close and personal to the farms and small towns that were scattered throughout downstate Illinois. Because of the lowered speed limit, Timothy had the window rolled down and was enjoying the sights and smells of the country. He had driven about four miles from a small town when he noticed the car was acting up. He knew he was less than an hour from Chicago and hoped the engine would hang on. His hope was short-lived, as a few minutes later everything in the car flashed for a moment and then it stalled. Timothy had enough momentum going to carry him a little further down the road and down the driveway of a farmhouse.

As he brought the car to a stop, Timothy saw an elderly man walk from the farmhouse to the barn. He thought the man had seen him, but he wasn't sure. Well, there was nothing to do but call dispatch and have them put him through to the garage. Picking up the radio, he pressed the button and got nothing but static. He tried again. Once again, there was no connection. He'd just have to find a phone.

He got out of the squad car and walked toward the barn. He opened the door and in the dim light saw row upon row of milking stalls. It must be a dairy farm, he reasoned. He called out to the farmer. "Hello, are you still in here?"

Waiting a few moments, he stepped further into the barn. The cement floor running down the middle of the barn was swept clean and fresh straw lay on the floors of each stall. Timothy took a deep breath. It smelled good, sweet straw, country air and a slight scent of manure. It reminded him of when he'd visited his grandparents in Ireland.

"Hello," he called out again. "I'm needing some help."

He turned and jumped, finding the elderly farmer standing just behind him. "Sorry," Timothy said, slightly embarrassed. "I guess I didn't hear you."

"You having problems with your car?" he asked.

Timothy nodded. “Yeah, I was wondering if I could use your phone and call for a wrecker?”

“Sure, there’s a phone in the corner, over there,” he said, pointing to a small room. “Would you like a glass of water?”

Timothy smiled and nodded. “That would be really nice,” he replied.

He walked over to the phone, pulled out the scrap of paper and dialed the number. “Hello, this is O’Reilly,” he said. “I’m having a bit of trouble with the squad.”

“It died on you, didn’t it?” the mechanic asked.

“Yes, but luckily I was on a country road, as you suggested,” he replied. “I’m on State Road 50, just north of Peotone.”

“Hey, I know that area, I grew up in Monee,” the mechanic said, naming a town only a few more miles up the road. “Where are you?”

“I’m at a small dairy farm,” Timothy said and then gave him the mileage from the last road he’d passed.

“Are you sure?” the mechanic asked.

“Yeah, I’m positive,” Timothy replied. “As soon as the squad started acting up, I made sure I paid attention to where I was so you could find me.”

"Okay," the mechanic said, his voice sounding strained. "You just hang tight. I'm going to bring the wrecker out there myself. I'll be there as soon as I can."

"Thanks," Timothy said, with a shrug. "I'll see you soon."

He hung up the phone and turned to see the farmer entering the barn with a glass of water in his hand.

"Here you are," the farmer said.

"Thank you," Timothy replied, taking a sip of the cool water. "That feels good on a hot day."

"Did you reach someone?" the farmer asked, nodding toward the phone.

"Aye, and they'll be out within the hour," he replied.

"We should push your car back out by the road," the farmer suggested. "That way he won't pass you by."

They walked out of the barn and toward the squad car. Timothy finished the last of the water in the cup and looked around for a place to put the empty glass.

"On the picnic table is fine," the farmer said, understanding his needs. "Now, you get in and I'll push."

Timothy looked at the diminutive man and shook his head. “No, I really think…”

“It’s downhill from the barn to the road,” the farmer said, cutting Timothy off. “It’s easier to have you steer and me push.”

Before he walked to the back of the car, the farmer took out an old handkerchief and wiped some of the grease from his hands. “Doing a little mechanical work,” he explained.

“Well, I surely appreciate your help,” Timothy replied.

With the farmer’s help, the squad car was at the side of the road in no time. Timothy got out of the car to thank the man, but he was already half-way down the drive heading toward the barn. “Thank you,” he called out anyway, before he climbed back into his car to wait.

Within record time Timothy saw the wrecker speeding up the road to meet him. The mechanic climbed out and quickly came over to Timothy’s car. “Let’s hurry and get you back to the station,” he said, pulling the tow chain down and slipping it under the body of the car. The squad was ready for transport within ten minutes.

“Wow, that was fast,” Timothy said.

“Yeah, I know,” the mechanic replied nervously. “Come on, let’s get the hell out of here.”

When they arrived at the garage, several members of the crew were waiting for them. The mechanic pulled the wrecker and the squad car into the garage and they both got out of the truck.

"So, did you talk to the farmer," one of the crew members asked, while the other chuckled beside him.

"What?" Timothy asked, confused.

"Shut up," the mechanic growled at the crew. "I don't want to go there."

"Go where?" Timothy asked. "Was there something wrong with the farmer? He seemed like a nice fellow to me."

The mechanic froze in his tracks and turned to Timothy. "You spoke to the farmer?" he asked slowly.

"Aye. He let me use his phone, gave me a glass of water and helped me push the squad to the road," he replied. "He was a good guy."

The mechanic stared at Timothy for several long moments and then finally said, his voice a hoarse whisper. "That farmer shot himself fifteen years ago, in the barn of that old farm," he said. "The property's been abandoned for eight years. No one can live there because it's haunted."

Chapter Four

"I didn't believe a word of it," Timothy said to his family in the flickering light of the Jack O'Lantern. "So the next day I drove back out to the farm with another officer. The road was thick with brush and overgrown. The milking parlor was filled with garbage and cobwebs. We pushed our way through the mess to the room with the phone. It too was covered with dust, except for the fingerprints that looked fresh. I picked up the phone and there was no dial tone."

He looked around the room at his family and nodded. "And as I walked out of the barn I spied the picnic table, now surrounded with tall weeds. But there in the middle was the glass I'd used the day before."

"Did they believe you?" Mary asked. "Back at the garage, did they believe you?"

"Aye, well they had no choice, did they?" he replied. "Because on the trunk of the squad were the greasy prints of the farmer's hand who pushed me down the lane."

"Whoa. Good story, Da," Tom said as he unwrapped a piece of candy and took a bite. "But, it's not as good as the one I have for tonight."

The father studied his son sternly for a moment and then a smile broke through the façade. "Ah, well, we'll see, won't we?" he asked with a nod.

Tom grinned. "We'll see and then you'll admit it," he replied. He stretched back on the couch, his long legs outstretched before him. The flickering light of the Jack O'Lantern only catching the lower portion of his face, leaving his eyes and forehead in the shadows. "Where do I begin?" he mused. "Well, I suppose at the very beginning. This was all Art's fault…"

"Wait! What?" Art exclaimed. "What are you talking about?"

Tom chuckled softly. "Well, if you'd pipe down, you'd know."

It was a bright, sunny summer day in the middle of August and the calendar in their bedroom reminded them that there were not going to be too many of them left. School was only weeks away and, as ten-year-old boys, they had an obligation to drain every moment of summer out of the time allotted.

Art coughed, a thick, raspy cough and grabbed a new tissue. Tom sighed deeply and clicked on the remote to see what else was on television.

"You don't have to stay in with me," Art told his twin. "Really, you could go out."

Tom turned and looked over his shoulder at his brother, laying on the living room couch with pillows behind him and a cotton blanket over him. "Really?" he asked.

There was silence in the room. They both knew the truth. As twins they had an unspoken communication. Art didn't want to be left alone in the house, but he felt obliged to offer Tom his freedom. Tom knew that Art didn't mean it, but he really hated missing a nice day.

Finally, Art sighed, a rumbling sigh that made him cough again. "Yeah, I mean it," he replied reluctantly. "No reason we both have to be miserable."

Tom didn't wait for Art to rethink his answer, he jumped to his feet and nodded. "Okay, I'm going," he said.

"Where are you going to go?" Art asked, wondering if he was just trying to punish himself even more by picturing his brother outside.

Tom shrugged. "I don't know," he said. "Probably the park. I could watch the baseball game."

Art coughed again and nodded. "Have fun," he said weakly.

Tom hurried out of the house, chased by his own guilt. Art would do the same, he reasoned, if things had been reversed. But he still kind of felt like a jerk. He kicked stones and grumbled to himself as he walked the three blocks over to the park. Sure enough, there was a baseball game being played and the scoreboard showed it was the bottom of the fourth inning.

Tom climbed up onto the bleachers and saw a group of friends from school. As he approached them, one of the girls, Nancy, looked up at him, shielding her eyes against the sun.

"Hey, which one are you?" she asked.

Used to the question, Tom shrugged. "I'm Tom," he said, finding a seat next to the group.

"Where's the other one?" she continued. "You two are never apart."

Guilt crept up again, Tom flushed and then he frowned, not too pleased about being reminded that he'd abandoned his brother. "He's sick," he snapped. "Okay?"

"Wow. Don't bite my head off," she quipped back, turning away from him and back to the game.

Tom grumbled and sat back against the metal bleacher. Why did everyone assume that he always had to be with Art, they weren't joined at the hip. The guilt continued to fester.

"Hey, O'Reilly, where's your other half?" one of the other boys asked when he noticed Tom had joined them.

Tom stood up. "You know, I can go out of the house without my brother," he exclaimed, then he turned around and hurried off the bleachers, jogging across the field and out of the park.

He didn't stop jogging until he came to the black wrought-iron fence of the old Tuberculosis Sanitarium. The 158 acres had been mostly converted by the city to a Nature Park, a Senior Living facility and some educational-use buildings, but there was still one old building hidden deep in the woods that remained. It was the old mansion house and it had housed the children's residence and everyone knew it was haunted.

Tom stared at the fence prohibiting entrance to this part of the acreage. He and Art had argued about checking out the old mansion a number of times. Art had always said it was too dangerous. Art was always the voice of reason. Always the fun-sucker. Tom looked up and down the street. There was no one around, no one to stop him. He'd show them. He'd show everyone that he didn't need his twin to have an adventure.

Pulling himself up onto the iron fence, he grabbed hold of a large tree limb that hung overhead. Wrapping his arms over it, he swung his body up and over the fence. He felt the tug and knew he'd caught the hem of his shorts on the pointed poles of the fencing. His arms were feeling the strain of holding all his weight and he knew if he didn't do something soon, he'd fall. He yanked his leg forward, heard the tear of material and then he was free. Scrambling onto the tree limb, he looked down at his short. They were torn nearly to his crotch. He sighed, Ma would not be happy about that.

Then he looked out into the acreage, the tree limb giving him an aerial view of the area. He could see the roof of the old building, its tiled roof cracked and broken with vegetation growing on top. He could also see an attic window through the break in the trees. It was dark and empty, but something about it caused a chill to run down his spine.

Maybe Art was right, maybe he shouldn't…

Tom shook his head. No! He was going to go on his own adventure and when he got home and told Art, he would be a hero.

He climbed down the old oak tree and made his way through the thick underbrush to the mansion house. The concrete steps leading up to the porch were cracked and crumbling. Weeds were growing on them and Tom had to push them aside to get up the stairs. The door had boards nailed over it with signs that read "No Trespassing." His heart thumped in his chest. Should he go in? He immediately heard his brother's voice in his mind telling him that it was against the law and he should turn around. That was the deciding point, he moved closer to the door.

Placing his hand on the old doorknob, he was surprised when it turned underneath his grip and that the door was unlocked. He jumped away, not sure what he wanted to do. The door slowly opened, the creak of the old hinges echoing inside the house. Tom swallowed nervously, then moved closer. The boards that had been nailed over the door crossed each other with just enough room for Tom to slip between them. He climbed through and found himself in the open lobby of the house. Most of the windows had been boarded up too, but there were cracks and holes where beams of light shone into the house.

He moved forward, dust motes flying all around him. The floor was tile and not fancy as he had expected. Instead it was gray-speckled flooring, like in an old hospital. Inside the house it smelled like mold and some medicine, like disinfectant. Tom wrinkled his nose at the smell, it was disgusting.

The staircase had a white painted banister, that was metal, and the paint was chipping off, leaving large patches of rust. The stairs, made out of the same tile as the floor, were sagging in the middle and he wondered if they would hold his weight. He walked to the foot of the stairs and looked up. The light from the doorway and the holes in the boards didn't reach to the second floor. All he could see was dark. He stared into the darkness, trying to talk himself into going up the stairs so he could tell Art.

"It's no big deal," he said aloud, the sound of his voice echoing in the hall. "No one's here."

The darkness above him changed, black over gray as a shadow glided across the top of the stairs. His heart in his throat, he stared up, his breath coming in gasps. Was it a cloud crossing over? Was it just his imagination?

Then the shadow reappeared, stopped at the top of the stairs and waited for a few moments. Then it started to descend. A cold chill swept over him and Tom's heart raced. He needed to get out of the old house and he needed to get out now!

He ran across the lobby and pushed himself out between the boards, scratching his exposed leg on a sharp piece of wood. He dropped onto the porch just as the heavy oak door slammed shut behind him. Scrambling back, on his hands and knees, he stumbled down the stairs and landed on the overgrown sidewalk. He looked up at the old house before him and his eyes caught a movement in the attic window. Dressed in a loose, white, hospital gown the young girl stared down at him for a long moment and then disappeared.

"You went there without me?" Art complained. "And you never told me?"

Tom shrugged, trying to ignore the goosebumps the memory evoked. "I really didn't want to talk about it," he explained. "I was really freaked out for a while."

"That was the year you didn't want to go to the haunted trail at the Nature Park," Sean said. "Now I understand why."

Tom nodded. "I thought for sure I'd see her walking around in her hospital gown," he said with a shudder.

"So that's how you ripped your shorts and cut your leg," Margaret added. "And you told me you'd played baseball and slid into third."

Tom nodded and looked a little embarrassed. "Yeah, sorry Ma," he said. "I should have told you."

She looked at him for a moment and then smiled. "Well, when we're frightened, we don't always tell our family about our experiences. Now do we?"

Chapter Five

"Well, that's a start to a story if I've ever heard one," Timothy said, turning to his wife. "What is it that you've never told your family?"

She smiled at him and shook her head. "Well, it's a secret I carried for a long time," she admitted. "And tonight's just as good a night as any to let you all know."

The grandfather clock was ticking loudly in the front hall, but the rest of the house was silent. She'd pushed a towel against the space between the floor and her door so her parents wouldn't see the light pooling out into the hallway. They'd warned her that taking the extra classes at school, along with her responsibilities at home, would be too much for her to handle. But she had argued and begged, promising that if it became too much of a burden, she'd let them know.

She rolled her head, stretching her neck muscles and working out the stiffness. She'd been stooped over the desk in her bedroom since after dinner trying to finish a term paper that was due the next day. The clock in the hall had just tolled one o'clock and she knew she'd have to be getting to bed soon if she was going to be able to function at all the next day. She looked down at the neat stack of typed papers on the corner of her desk. She only had the references to type and then she'd be done.

She reached for the glass of milk on the other side of the desk, picked it up and found, to her disappointment, that it was empty. She debated for a moment. She had about a half-hour's worth of work to do, she probably had enough energy without another glass of milk. Then she remembered the spicy gingerbread cake her mother had made that evening and the decision was made. A piece of cake and a glass of milk would be just what she needed to refresh her body and help her finish her work.

Picking up the glass, she flicked off the overhead light in her bedroom, slowly opened the door and slipped into the dark hallway. They lived in the country, so there were no streetlights shining in from outside to illuminate the house. Only a few well-placed nightlights that cast a soft-glow in the shadowed darkness. She was nearly to the kitchen when she noticed the figure sitting on the couch in the living room. Startled at first, it took her only a moment to realize who it was.

"Grandpa," she whispered, hurrying to his side. "I didn't know you were coming? Do Ma and Da know you're here?"

He smiled at her and shook his head.

"Should I wake them?" she asked. "I know Ma would want to make up a bed for you."

He shook his head again. “I’m fine,” he whispered back to her.

As the only granddaughter, she had enjoyed a special relationship with her grandfather. They often went hiking or fishing together. He would tell her stories about his youth and she would tell him of her challenges at school. They would often raid her mother’s pantry and remain silent in an unspoken pact when there were questions about missing cookies or pastries. Although she was quite sure her Ma had figured it out long ago.

“How are you darling?” he asked.

“I’m good, Grandpa,” she replied. “I’m finishing up my paper. I only have the references to go.”

“There’s me brilliant granddaughter,” he said, standing and enfolding her in his arms.

She sighed happily. There was nothing like a hug from her grandfather.

“I love you, darling,” he whispered to her. “And I’ve always been so proud of you.”

She looked up into his familiar eyes and her heart filled. “I love you too, grandpa,” she said.

He hugged her once more and then stepped back. “Now, get your treats and off with you to finish your paper,” he said. “Make me proud.”

She nodded. “I will. I promise.”

“Aye, you always do.”

She filled her milk cup, cut a piece of gingerbread and, with a quick wave in her grandfather’s direction, hurried back to her room to finish the paper.

Her alarm woke her bright and early the next morning. She stumbled from bed and headed down the hall toward the bathroom.

“Darling, could you come to the kitchen for a moment?” her mother called.

Nodding sleepily, she changed directions and headed into the kitchen, glancing over towards the couch to see if her grandfather was awake.

“You won’t be going to school today,” her mother said as she entered the kitchen.

“Why not?” she asked, clearly confused.

Then she noticed that her mother’s eyes were red-rimmed and filled with tears. “Ma, what’s wrong?” she asked.

“Your Auntie called this morning,” her mother explained. “Your grandfather passed away last night.”

Fully awake now, her eyes widened and she shook her head. "No, that can't be true," she said. "Last night..."

But before she could finish, her mother interrupted her. "It was just before one o'clock," she explained, her voice catching. "Your auntie was in the room with him. It was a peaceful parting."

She glanced over at the couch, then back at her mother and was about to explain when she thought better of it. She'd asked him if he wanted her to wake her parents and he'd said no. It was his final gift to her and she would cherish it forever.

Margaret wiped the tears away that had slipped on to her cheeks. "I never shared this with anyone," she said. "Until today."

Timothy put his arm around her shoulders and pulled her close. "It was a special moment," he said. "A sacred moment. Thank you for sharing it."

She nodded. "He was a great man," she said, looking over at her husband. "And I know he would have loved you."

He kissed her forehead and hugged her again. "Thank you for that," he whispered to her. Then he turned to Mary. "It's your turn now."

"Really? After that story?" Mary asked, wiping away her own tears. "Well, that's not fair."

"All's fair in love and ghost stories," Art inserted. "Go for it, little sister."

Mary sighed. "Okay, but my story does not have warm fuzzies like Ma's."

Chapter Six

Mary O'Reilly watched as the car pulled away from the curb and headed down the street. She felt her heart drop, watching her parents drive away from the Sorority house. Her new lodging for the school year. She stepped away from the window and looked at the boxes, tubs and suitcases all lined up on top of and next to her narrow bed. With a resigned sigh, she rolled up her sleeves and started unpacking all of her belongings.

She was in the bathroom, storing her toiletries in her cabinet when she heard the crash. Fearing the worst, she stuffed her remaining items onto the shelf and rushed back into the bedroom. Confused, she slowly examined the room. Nothing was out of place. Nothing was on the floor. Nothing could have caused that sound.

With a shrug, she went back into the bathroom. To her surprise, the items she'd shoved on the shelf were all arranged neatly in order. "Did I do that?" she asked herself.

She finished up in the bathroom, stacked all of her tubs and suitcases together to be put in the house's basement and finally made her bed. Examining her half of the room with a critical eye, she smiled. It looked organized and homey. She nodded. Yeah, she could be happy here for the next four months.

Dragging the tubs and suitcases into the hall, she locked her door and then headed across the hall to the staircase to carry the empty containers down three flights of stairs to the basement. Piling the containers on top of each other, Mary lifted them in her arms, the containers blocking her vision, and slowly slid her foot forward to feel her way onto the first step down.

The slight nudge between her shoulder blades knocked her forward. She gasped in fear as she felt herself falling headfirst down the stairs. But before she could even emit of scream of terror, strong hands grabbed her shoulders and pulled her back, setting her upright. "Thank you," she stuttered, her heart in her throat.

She turned to meet her rescuer and was shocked to see that she was the only one there. "Hello?" she called out, wondering if her rescuer had slipped into one of the nearby rooms. She placed the containers on the floor and walked down the hall. "Hello?" she called again. There was no response.

"Okay, that was weird," she said, taking a deep breath to calm her nerves. "That was really weird."

She started to pick up the containers again, when she was interrupted, but this time in a more normal way. "Hey, I can help you with those," a friendly voice sailed up from below her. "You don't want to come down these stairs blindly."

Mary put the containers down once again and smiled at the young woman walking up the stairs. "Hi," she said with a quick shrug and then she nodded toward the pile on the floor next to her. "They're not really heavy, just cumbersome. I can carry them, really."

The young woman finished the climb up the stairs and shook her head. "It's not how heavy they are," she said. "It's…" She paused and bit her lower lip, debating her next words. "Okay, don't judge me. But weird stuff happens on this floor and, really, you don't want to go down those stairs and not being able to see."

Mary shook her head. "I'm not going to judge you at all," Mary replied. "Especially since I nearly took a facer down the stairs just a few moments ago."

"Someone push you?" the girl asked.

"Yeah," Mary said. "I felt hands on my back. But, just as weird, someone caught me and pulled me back up."

The girl sighed. "Well, at least you've got someone on your side."

"Someone on my side?" Mary asked. "What does that mean?"

"Back in the seventies there was a fire in the house," she explained. "They say it was bad wiring, but no one really knows. Anyway, most of the girls were able to get out, but three of the girls got caught in their room. The fire was between them and the staircase, and the fire department didn't have a ladder tall enough to reach the third floor."

"Oh, that's terrible," Mary said.

"Yeah, it really sucked," the girl said. "But now the girls play pranks on the sorority sisters that live in the house. And…" She paused and looked apologetically at Mary. "They really like to pick on the newbies."

"Great," Mary replied. "So, one of them tried to push me down the staircase and another one saved me, right?"

The girl nodded and smiled. "And the third one offered to help you carry your stuff down the stairs."

And then she disappeared.

"Whoa!" Sean called out. "I didn't see that coming."

Mary grinned. "Yeah, neither did I."

"So, what did you do?" Art asked. "I mean, with your stuff?"

"I slowly dragged it down the staircase, one hand on the railing, the other hand pulling the stuff down after me," she said. "And I didn't have a good night's sleep in that room for the entire semester."

"I slowly dragged it down the staircase, one hand on the railing, the other hand pulling the stuff down after me," she said. "And I didn't have a good night's sleep in that room for the entire semester."

"What is it about staircases?" Art asked.

"What do you mean?" Margaret countered.

Art shrugged and looked around the room at his family. "Well, I guess it's time for my story."

Chapter Seven

The library was quiet, which was precisely the reason Art O'Reilly chose it. Many of his roommates were on sports scholarships and, in this university at least, it meant that they had no fear of the approaching midterms. As long as they performed on the field, they and their scholarships were just fine. So, his room and the rooms surrounding it were filled with loud music, parties and an overall atmosphere not conducive to studying.

Art had found a small desk and chair that were nearly hidden in the far corner of the book stacks of the library. The books around him were old law journals and case studies, which were now available online, so he rarely was disturbed by another student. Just behind him was a staircase to a loft area that held reference books, but that staircase was off limits to students. Art felt he had found the perfect hidey-hole.

His stomach growled and, first looking around carefully to be sure no one was close, Art reached down into his backpack and pulled out a bag containing a submarine sandwich and some chips and placed it on the desk. He knew eating was strictly forbidden in the library, but he had four more chapters to study and didn't have time to go out and eat, and then get back to the library before it closed.

He took a large bite of the sandwich, drank from his water bottle and resumed his studies.

Lost in a particular case study, Art was surprised when he heard the clicking sounds of the banks of lights being turned off. He glanced at his phone and realized it was ten minutes past closing time. He wrapped up the remains of his dinner and stuffed it into his backpack, along with his notepad and books, and started to hurry towards the circulation desk. The library was dark, but the large picture windows along the wall allowed the light from the campus streetlamps to flow through. Art could see his way through the tall rows of shelves and around the tables toward the front of the library. When he reached the circulation desk, he discovered it was empty. He slowly scanned the library, looking for an employee, but couldn't see anyone. He walked over to the door, but it was locked tight.

He started to pull out his phone, to call security to let him out, and then had second thoughts. He pictured his dorm room and the party that would certainly be occurring and realized that being locked in the library could be the best thing that could happen to him.

With a resigned shrug, he turned around and walked back to the desk and chair hidden in the back of the library. Looking around the area, he discovered a light switch that turned on shelving lighting, illuminating the titles of the law books. He moved his desk and chair closer to the stacks to take advantage of their miniscule glow. He pulled the remains of his dinner back out of his backpack, took another bite, and then pulled out his book. In a few minutes, he was once again absorbed in details of a case study.

He wasn't sure what made him look up from his book. Maybe it was the sudden drop in temperature in the room. Maybe it was a shadow crossing over the desk. Maybe it was his sixth sense. But whatever the reason, Art lifted his eyes from the book and looked over at the staircase that led to the loft. But this time, the staircase wasn't empty.

The woman wore a white blouse and long skirt. Her hair was pulled up in a bun on the top of her head. She walked slowly up the stairs, as if she was carrying a heavy load of books. And Art could see right through her.

His heart hammered in his throat as he watched her glide slowly up the steps in an even motion. Then, once at the top of the steps, she stopped and turned. She looked down from her vantage place, above him and her eyes met his.

Art felt his blood run cold. He was transfixed in his chair, barely able to breath and not able to move. The ghost moved, as if to put down the stack of books, then she walked to the railing of the loft and met Art's eyes once again.

"Shhhhhhhhhh!" she whispered, the sound sending chills up Art's spine. Then she disappeared.

Art stared at the spot for several long minutes, too frightened to move. He quickly stuffed everything into his backpack and, keeping his eyes on the staircase, backed away from his desk and chair. Finally, when he reached the narrow aisle between the stacks, he ran towards the circulation desk and the front door.

He knew he'd have to call security. He knew the door was locked. But all he could think about was getting out of the library. When he reached the door, he heard the mechanic click of the door being unlocked and then he was sure he heard a soft chuckle.

He grabbed the handle, pulled the door open and dashed out of the library into the night air. He didn't slow down until he'd reached the bright lights and noise of his dormitory.

"Did you ever see her again?" Mary asked.

"Why don't you ask him if he ever entered the library again," Tom teased.

Art grinned. "No to both questions," he admitted. "I don't think I've ever been as frightened in my entire life."

“Good story, lad,” Timothy said. “And a fine way to end the night.” He leaned forward and blew out the candle in the Jack O’Lantern.

Chapter Eight

The house was quiet and all of the children had found their way back to the bedrooms they used as children. The Jack O'Lantern had been moved to the kitchen counter to cool down before it was thrown away. The bowl of candy was now nearly filled with empty wrappers and the dishwasher was humming away.

Margaret O'Reilly made sure the back door was locked and then switched off the kitchen light. The few, well-placed nightlights illuminated the hallway and the living room as she made her way to the staircase. Suddenly she stopped and turned toward the couch.

A dark shadow sat perched on the edge of the couch in the darkened room and, rather than being afraid, she smiled.

"How are you grandpa?" she asked softly. "I hope you enjoyed the stories."

The shadowed figure did not speak, but merely nodded his head in assent.

"Good," Maggie replied. "I'd hoped you would. Good night."

She turned and made her way up the stairs, while the shadowed figure slowly faded away.

The End

Notes from the author:

I hope you enjoy this new collection of ghost stories shared by the O'Reilly family. I love that it's not only become a tradition with the O'Reillys, but also with many of my readers around the world. There is nothing better than sitting around a cozy room telling stories that will make you shiver and also make you wonder about those little sounds you hear in your house when no one else is home.

For more ghost stories, please visit my website – www.terrireid.com - and you'll find a collection of stories in my Freaky Friday section. There's a new ghost story every week and even a comment section where you can share your own.

Happy Halloween!!

Terri Reid

About the author: Terri Reid lives near Freeport, the home of the Mary O'Reilly Mystery Series, and loves a good ghost story. An independent author, Reid uploaded her first book "Loose Ends – A Mary O'Reilly Paranormal Mystery" in August 2010. By the end of 2013, "Loose Ends" had sold over 200,000 copies. She has sixteen other books in the Mary O'Reilly Series, the first books in the following series - "The Blackwood Files," "The Order of Brigid's Cross," and "The Legend of the Horsemen." She also has a stand-alone romance, "Bearly in Love." Reid has enjoyed Top Rated and Hot New Release status in the Women Sleuths and Paranormal Romance category through Amazon US. Her books have been translated into Spanish, Portuguese and German and are also now also available in print and audio versions. Reid has been quoted in a number of books about the self-publishing industry including "Let's Get Digital" by David Gaughran and "Interviews with Indie Authors: Top Tips from Successful Self-Published Authors" by Claire and Tim Ridgway. She was also honored to have some of her works included in A. J. Abbiati's book "The NORTAV Method for Writers – The Secrets to Constructing Prose Like the Pros."

She loves hearing from her readers at author@terrireid.com

Other Books by Terri Reid:

Mary O'Reilly Paranormal Mystery Series:

Loose Ends (Book One)

Good Tidings (Book Two)

Never Forgotten (Book Three)

Final Call (Book Four)

Darkness Exposed (Book Five)

Natural Reaction (Book Six)

Secret Hollows (Book Seven)

Broken Promises (Book Eight)

Twisted Paths (Book Nine)

Veiled Passages (Book Ten)

Bumpy Roads (Book Eleven)

Treasured Legacies (Book Twelve)

Buried Innocence (Book Thirteen)

Stolen Dreams (Book Fourteen)

Haunted Tales (Book Fifteen)

Deadly Circumstances (Book Sixteen)

Frayed Edges (Book Seventeen)

Mary O'Reilly Short Stories

The Three Wise Guides

Tales Around the Jack O'Lantern 1

Tales Around the Jack O'Lantern 2

The Order of Brigid's Cross (Sean's Story)

Made in the USA
San Bernardino, CA
02 October 2016